SPIES GO RUNNING

KX4, a new and deadly germ warfare discovery, has been hijacked by Arab guerilla leader El Dashiki. Israel is in grave danger and British agent Marieanne Payne is ordered to recover the stolen bacteria. She approaches Hitchin Smith, a millionaire gunrunner, who unwittingly agrees to her proposition, eager to prolong his affair with the beautiful Marieanne. But she takes him deeper into danger and the Middle Eastern conflict until finally her search for KX4 explodes into open warfare.

Books by Olga Quinn
in the Linford Mystery Library:

SPIES ON THE ROOF

OLGA QUINN

SPIES GO RUNNING

Complete and Unabridged

LINFORD
Leicester

First published in Great Britain in 1971 by
Robert Hale Limited
London

First Linford Edition
published 2004
by arrangement with
Robert Hale Limited
London

British Library CIP Data

Quinn, Olga
   Spies go running.—Large print ed.—
Linford mystery library
1. Bioterrorism—Fiction 2. Women spies—
Fiction 3. Middle East—Fiction 4. Spy stories
5. Large type books
I. Title
823.9'14 [F]

ISBN 1–84395–540–7

Published by
F. A. Thorpe (Publishing)F
Anstey, Leicestershire

Set by Words & Graphics Ltd.
Anstey, Leicestershire
Printed and bound in Great Britain by
T. J. International Ltd., Padstow, Cornwall

This book is printed on acid-free paper

1

Marieanne raised her foot from the accelerator and steered the Citroën into the self-service station. It was deserted; cool night air greeted her as she stepped out. One-thirty a.m: a completely insane time to go to work. But Sir John didn't recall a top-grade agent to discuss the weather: somewhere and somehow a very large balloon had gone up.

She fed a note into the hungry mechanism, started to fill the tank, and looked up as a large black Daimler pulled in at the far end of the pumps. The warning system, perfected by years of use, instinctively nudged her brain. Every nerve tensed and an unpleasant coldness clawed the back of her neck. She wasn't armed. The gun was clipped under the driver's seat as her dress provided no cover for a holster. Besides, she hadn't expected trouble.

The two occupants of the Daimler were

walking towards her. Marieanne released the pump grip and moved to the front of the car. But, as her fingers slid beneath the seat, a sharp and familiar pain jabbed into her back. A hand passed hers and pulled out the automatic.

'Just fill the tank, Mrs Payne, then you will take a passenger — for a short drive.'

She turned slowly. They were middle-eastern, possibly Egyptian. The man who had spoken pocketed her gun. He was large and flabby, with a small moustache, and appeared to be hot from the way he dabbed his forehead with a handkerchief. It was the second man, a slimmer, middle-aged individual, who held the gun.

She walked back to the pump. They followed, stood between the two cars and watched her. The fat man took two cigars from his pocket and handed one to the other Arab. The gun still covered her.

Then their heads were huddled close as he lit the cigars and, in that second, Marieanne realised she *was* armed. She pulled the nozzle from the tank. The Arab's lighter was still held against his companion's cigar and the fuel met the small flame with a crisp whoosh and a hot, smoky blaze that immediately enveloped them. Screaming, they fell to the ground and threshed wildly about.

Marieanne dropped the pump and climbed back into the front of the Citroën. As her hand pressed against the starter she looked back at the appalling scene through the mirror.

'You could have at least introduced yourselves,' she muttered.

After driving for about a mile she stopped by a phone box and reported the fire.

It was a fine night and the roads were clear. She threw the sage-green DS 19 round bends and corners, treating the sharp air brake with contempt, and drove as fast as she dared.

As London grew close she thought of the two men she had incinerated. They had been an occupational hazard, dealt with by the only means possible at the time. But, what a horrible way to die, she told herself. Her husband had burned to death little more than a year before. The airliner he was travelling back to London on had been blasted to pieces over the Austrian Alps — with the compliments of the Russian Secret Service — a gesture of their thoughts on the disservice he had just rendered them. Bob Payne had also been a top-grade agent, and seventy-seven people, mostly returning holidaymakers, had died with him.

Marieanne began to feel a little sick and took one hand from the wheel, pressing it hard against her stomach.

★　★　★

As she walked into the outer office, the 'enter' sign flashed from the wall. It was almost four a.m. She crossed the room; the double soundproof doors opened. Johnny Armstrong smiled his welcome, but she took the brandy he offered without looking at him.

Sir John greeted her.

'Sit down,' he invited, but she declined. She had battled with the chairs in the Master's office for too many years. Either she had to perch on the edge like a parrot, in order that her feet should touch the floor, or sit erect against the hard, high carved back and let her feet dangle.

She leaned against the filing cabinet, savouring the mellow liquor, and looked around the room and at the two men who patiently awaited her pleasure. She was tense and rubbed her forehead with unsteady fingers. The clock struck the hour and she sighed.

Johnny stood by the window. He was five-foot six and slimly built — with a degree of good looks that could only be called beauty. The fine and sensual features, exposing the artistic side of his nature, only thinly veiled his natural cynicism.

He wore a light beige suit, lime-green crepe shirt and a broad mauve tie. His longish mid-brown hair was thick and the waves and curls tumbled in skilfully cut profusion. It would have been stylish and envied on a woman; on Johnny it complemented his features and taste in clothes.

His deep-green eyes were fixed on Marieanne. He hadn't left her since her last assignment in Tibet. They had lived together as they had before her marriage, but it was a relationship constantly interrupted by the nature of their work and temperaments. Four days previous he had sarcastically ridiculed her feelings for the Russian agent she had worked with in Tibet. Marieanne had lost her temper and driven down to the Wye Valley for what was to have been a week's holiday with her father.

Johnny was still on active field service but had become, more or less, the Master's right-hand man. It was obvious that, one day, he would sit behind Sir John's desk. He had the same skills and years of practical experience that the Master had notched up before, and during, the last war. And now there were the special duties that singled him out from the other top-grade operators: he often had to check and tighten up the overseas stations: he had become the official mopper-up and coverer-up of messy situations: agents who turned bad he disposed of; those who became suspect he checked on by devious snooping and prying: he was a master of bribery and blackmail; a skilled engineer of compromising situations. To Marieanne, though, he was gradually becoming a 'yes' man — a whipping-boy for Sir John, and she didn't like that. At times she almost despised him for it.

Sir John stroked his wiry beard and began the long, laborious process of lighting his noisy old pipe.

Marieanne wondered whether he ever went home to sleep like other human beings — if indeed he was human. Even Johnny looked as if it were the middle of the day.

She stepped forward, lightly tapping her fingers against the fine glass.

'And what is the latest 'in' grudge the Middle East is holding against us?' she asked.

The brandy had anaesthetised her earlier emotions and her cheeks felt warm and glowing. The tension and unsteadiness had gone.

'Why do you ask that?' The Master raised disorderly brows.

'Because I had to set fire to two Arabs

just outside Oxford on the way here. They seemed intent on taking me for a short drive in the country. No doubt it would have been my last.'

She related the fire-lighting act.

There was a short silence until Johnny muttered:

'Jesus!'

'They didn't give their names — but *he* definitely wasn't one of them.'

'Describe them,' Sir John demanded.

She prowled back and forth across the room, quickly creating a word picture of the two men. Johnny and the Master watched, both aware of the strength of mind and body Marieanne possessed: she didn't quite reach five-foot three and weighed under seven and a half stone, but her skill at karate and judo made her small build no disadvantage and she could floor a man twice her weight with ease.

'Sit down,' Sir John repeated. 'You'll wear out the carpet.'

She sat down and he picked up one of the many phones from the desk.

'There's been an incident at a self-service petrol station on the other side of

Oxford. Two men were burnt — to death I would imagine. From the description we have, it would appear they were the two Egyptians we've had our eye on for some time. Follow it up then classify it as a purely Departmental matter. Stop all Police investigations immediately.'

There was a short pause, then he went on:

'Yes, one of ours . . . A green Citroën DS 19 . . . Mrs Payne's . . . That's right — no further action at all to be taken.'

He put the phone down and smiled faintly at Marieanne.

'Well, that's that. Quite an unpleasant way to die. I must say I'm rather surprised at their tenacity: not only are they ridding us of our agents in the Arab States — they're trying it here as well.'

'What's happened?'

'A lot of things.' He sat back heavily in the large, old swivel chair that clanked and groaned under his gradually increasing weight and gazed around the office. It had the mellowed atmosphere of dark wood, old leather, and the musty smell of tobacco. It never altered: the carpet, furnishings, fittings and decorations were just the same as they had been the first time Johnny and Marieanne had entered it. Only the Master changed, and the years were eroding him into old age. His blue eyes alone remained young and flashed like marbles, but his hair and beard were greyer — and sparser, and the once-rosy cheeks had paled and sagged.

'Ring down for coffee, Armstrong. Marieanne looks tired.'

She *was* tired and knew Sir John was about to career into a long-drawn-out revelation of facts, abbreviated with many pauses and pipe-lighting sessions. It would go on for hours and this wasn't the time of day to be subjected to such an ordeal. She sat back, tensed her arms and fingers in front of her for a few seconds, then relaxed.

He began:

'Our highly respected boffins at Porton Down have come up with the discovery of a lifetime, Marieanne.' Sarcasm edged every word. 'British scientists are the proud discoverers of the new super improved germ named KX4 that has extra-quick-action properties and kills over ninety-five per cent of those infected.'

'Sounds a wonderful idea,' Marieanne commented. 'Should sell well with advertising copy like that. Maybe those great and beneficent men will get the Nobel Peace Prize . . . '

' . . . Or even a Duke of Edinburgh Award,' Johnny cut in. He handed her a cigarette and lit it. She was suddenly deeply conscious of him as his slender hand was close to her face. His manicured fingers held the thin gold lighter she had bought years before. She was tempted to touch his hand, knowing it would be cool and smooth, and the familiar tangy perfume she was so accustomed to conjured up ten thousand memories of their lives together. She looked up and his eyes smiled at her from under long, dark lashes.

'What has all this to do with the Arabs?' she asked, turning back to the Master.

'Porton Down has lost a batch of KX4 and we have information that their loss is the Arabs' gain.'

'Then Israel is due for a heavy epidemic of something or other.'

'That is probable. I expect you know something of the germ-warfare industry.'

She sighed.

'I've read about it; seen programmes on TV about it, and once had the rather dubious honour of being shown around Porton.'

She knew she was still going to hear the history of germs from A to Z regardless, and stifled back a yawn.

The green light above the door flashed and Sir John pressed a button on his desk. A bleary-eyed night clerk entered with a tray containing one battered flask, three mugs, a handful of sugar lumps, and three nasty plastic teaspoons that could easily have been the nesting place for the missing batch of KX4. He put the tray down on the desk, then left.

Sir John blew his nose, cleared his throat, then commenced:

'KX4 is a completely new type of plague. Over the past few years Porton has experimented with, and produced, many germs: germs for pneumonic plague, bubonic plague, cholera, anthrax, and smallpox. All of these are extremely effective, with a ninety to one hundred per cent death rate in most cases. But germs can have disadvantages when you want to take over the country you have infected as the infection often lingers for long periods of time. An experiment carried out on an uninhabited Scottish island proved that anthrax can render an area infectious for a hundred years. But the great advantage of germ warfare is that all one needs to do is start the ball rolling, then the filthy little microbes do the rest. KX4 is a marvel and has the best of both worlds, so to speak. Its death rate is, as I said before, over ninety-five per cent and the symptoms are virtually undetectable for about twelve hours; then the victim is suddenly brought down in an intense, rapidly increasing fever; he becomes semi-conscious and is dead within five or six hours. But now we come to the big selling point of this particular germ: when the plague has wiped out all contacts, the infection dies off more or less immediately. So, as soon as the last victim has died and no fresh outbreaks occur, it would be quite safe to close in and do the quick takeover bit. There is no antidote yet: that is still in process of being discovered.'

Marieanne poured the coffee and handed it round while Sir John continued:

'Anyway, a few months ago it was decided to transfer some of Porton's work. They're churning out bugs by the million — by what amounts to nothing more than assembly-line processes. But some of their latest experiments are extremely dangerous when one considers how close they are to habitation.'

'They have seven hundred acres surrounding them,' Marieanne cut in. 'Isn't that enough — or are they now in the market for giant super-sized bugs with twelve legs?'

'Public opinion has had a lot to do with it. You know — letters to the papers, M.P.s asking questions in the House, and deputations to Ministers and local Mayors. Eventually the powers that be decided to transfer the whole department that deals with these particularly deadly experiments.'

'Where to?' she asked.

'Western Australia: a new experimental station has been built hundreds of miles from any civilisation.'

Johnny gave a snide laugh:

'Obviously the powers that be care little for the welfare of our meat-pie-eating friends down under.'

Ignoring the interruption, the Master continued:

'Two days ago a transporter flew out with the entire Department's equipment and bacteria, which included, of course, a canister containing KX4. They had their own security arrangements but we put a man on duty at each touchdown. Peter Carlyle was at Beirut: he was found dead next morning, by which time the plane was almost at Western Australia. The freight was checked immediately. There was still a canister, but close examination revealed it to be an exact duplicate containing jelly similar to the nutritive jelly the germs feed on — but there were no germs. The batch of KX4 had obviously been stolen at Beirut.'

Utmost in Marieanne's mind was the dead agent. She always had a morbid interest in how the others died and felt it gave some indication of what the gods would favour as her fate — if violence was to end her life.

'What happened to Carlyle?'

'He was strangled . . . '

'Garrotted with a piece of wire, darling,' John chipped in. 'Almost decapitated, I believe.'

That lowered the odds a little from the usual quick and civilised bullet. She winced inwardly. Carlyle had been a top-grade agent for five years; a likeable guy, married with three children.

'Who has the germs, sir?'

She pushed her thoughts away into the little emotion box at the back of her mind. It was a little-used box, usually kept tightly shut and locked, but it contained gems that she sometimes let run through the sensitive fingers of her mind: there were gems of life with Johnny — long before the dirt of Service work; gems of a short, unconventional but

16

happy marriage, and of a fleeting but deep affair with the Russian, Kondrashin.

Sir John was struggling with his pipe again and it hissed and gurgled as he used countless matches. His bright blue eyes watched her but she had to wait until the pipe was lit and half his coffee consumed.

'El Dashiki,' he finally said. 'The latest thorn in the side of Israel and leader of one of the forces of Fedayeen: they are the 'men of sacrifice' dedicated to smash the Jews. So far, Arafat's El Fatah organisation has held the position as the largest guerrilla force. El Fatah, as you know, is based in Jordan and Lebanon and is very well armed, with such handy little things as Kalashnikov assault rifles and 122mm. long-range heavy guns — all, of course, manufactured in the Soviet Union. El Dashiki or Yasir Abu-Hashi, to use his real name, started his force late in 1967 in Lebanon after spending a few years as a successful international criminal. His group is gathered in the far south-east close to the Israeli border. But it has been losing many men in border attacks and its

17

fast-growing ranks, gathered from the hordes of Palestinian refugees and pro-Nasser Syrians, are outstripping their meagre recources of arms.'

'Why the name El Dashiki?' Marieanne asked.

'Because he always wears a dashiki, of course,' Johnny answered. 'You know — one of those African poncho-type jerkins.'

'Oh, pardon my ignorance!'

The Master continued:

'We have been told El Dashiki has the germs. Our source of information was very expensive but has always proved reliable. He is quite capable of carrying off such a stunt. He's half Arab and half negro — Egyptian father and Congolese mother. Went to the U.S.S.R. twelve years ago and was trained in Intelligence and subversive activities in Moscow for five years. But something happened that landed him in mild disgrace with the Russians and he was kicked out of the Soviet Union. Maybe that's the reason why the Russians have discouraged Arab States from supplying arms to him. Also,

I don't think, from a publicity angle, they like the idea of someone so closely linked with themselves, not to mention international crime, being involved in direct warfare against Israel. He has arms, some of them Russian, but not enough for his mission and he is losing them every time he loses a man.'

Again the pipe had expired.

'Through their constant attacks,' he eventually said, 'all the Fedayeen groups are goading the Jews into bitter and, of late, unreasonably violent revenge. Any official pressure on Nasser and other Arab leaders to stop aggression and negotiate terms with Israel should be blown sky high if Israel were to become the demon king in the pantomime: it would put America and the West in an extremely awkward position as we have to uphold Israel's right to exist.

'El Dashiki's Soviet training, plus his possible possession of KX4, could bring Israel to her knees. Then, with sufficient arms, he could take over the whole country. If substantially armed, he might be able to persuade many of Arafat's supporters to join him and also take over some of the smaller Fedayeen groups. It would put him on a mighty high pedestal in the eyes of the Arab people if he crushed Israel. Moscow would soon forget his misdemeanours and the Middle East would become his oyster.'

Marieanne stubbed out her cigarette.

'Which one of us is to find the germs?'

'You will find the germs, Marieanne; Johnny will be on the case — in the background.'

She wondered why she had bothered to ask as, recently, Johnny had acquired the habit of being 'in the background' while she was up front facing all the hazards.

'I don't think El Dashiki will want to part with his germs,' she commented.

'He needs arms desperately,' Sir John answered. 'If he doesn't get them soon he'll be obliged to do a deal and join up with some other guerrilla group. But that would be the last resort — being a typical Arab, El Dashiki trusts no one and would be very reluctant either to share or lose his power. He wants to be top dog himself.

'So, we are going to see that he gets his arms — and pays for them. While he is busy playing with his new toys you will find KX4. What happens to him and his group afterwards depends. It would be desirable, of course, for them never to have the opportunity of using the weapons. There is no margin for error in this job. At some stage or other El Dashiki will probably possess both the arms and the germs. At that stage of the proceedings he will be an extremely dangerous man.'

Again Sir John lapsed into silence to allow his words to digest. Marieanne was tired. Johnny sat behind her, continually stretching and snapping the bracelet of his watch against his wrist.

'Have you heard of Hitchin Smith?' the Master asked.

'Hitchin Smith . . . the gunrunner?' she offered.

'Yes. He arrived in London yesterday from Portofino, where there'd been some trouble over a woman. He's staying at the Hilton and you, Marieanne, must see to it that he agrees to do a deal with El

Dashiki. We'll put a large consignment of arms at his disposal. He's just made himself a pile out of a Central African State and, if he follows his usual pattern, will now want a few weeks' holiday and rest. So your offer has to be very inviting as we can't afford for him to take his rest.'

It was increasingly difficult to keep awake. She yawned, rubbed her face, and her eyelids continually slipped heavily over tired eyes. Johnny sensed her problem and poured more coffee.

'You should have no difficulty in persuading him to mix business with pleasure.' He smiled knowingly at her.

'You will accompany Smith to El Dashiki,' Sir John said. 'Your identity will be changed, of course.'

'What if he knows I'm an agent — those two recognised me easily enough tonight.'

'Yes, but they have been snooping round London for close on two years. I doubt very much if El Dashiki has a picture book of British secret agents.'

He pushed a manilla envelope across the crowded desk.

'These are photographs of Smith. Some of them were taken at Portofino over the past few days with the reason for the trouble, Signora Picone. You'll notice that he now sports one of those ridiculous moustaches that are all the rage.'

He looked up:

'I'm surprised you haven't got one, Armstrong. You don't usually miss out on all these damn fool trends.'

'Me, sir? Oh, I'm far too lovely for a moustache!'

The Master smiled. Armstrong's looks, plus the mannerisms he had perfected, made him a natural in the role of a homosexual — a part which proved extremely useful on many occasions in the course of his work. But his appearance, like Marieanne's, was a complete misconception.

Marieanne looked through the photographs. Hitchin Smith was tall — at least six feet, and slim, with a flamboyant taste in clothes. But, whereas Johnny's clothes and appearance gave the impression of him being camp, Hitchin Smith radiated hypermasculinity. His black hair was long in the neck and unruly. The Mexican moustache Marieanne liked: all he needed to complete the picture was a sombrero, crossed bandoleers, and fancy firearms. And she rather liked his dark, sleepy eyes. Smith was very attractive, with a broad smile and tanned skin that accentuated the whiteness of his well-formed teeth. She knew he was a rogue with a good sense of humour.

Sleep still tried to overpower her as the Master extolled Smith's abilities as a salesman and runner of guns. She stood, crossed to the window, and pushed her dark hair behind her ears. Dawn was beginning to light the sky.

'I don't like working with amateurs, sir; it's dangerous.' She turned to Johnny for support, but he gave her none.

'They always do such bloody stupid things,' she went on, and was about to ramble off into instances when Johnny interrupted.

'Smith's no fool, Marieanne. From what I know of him, he's a pretty shrewd guy.'

'At selling guns, maybe,' she argued,

'but amateurs have nearly cost me my life on more than one occasion — and yours as well.'

'Then you will just have to be that little bit more careful, won't you, darling?'

Sir John added his assurances:

'We need Smith for this operation. I don't suppose anyone has much admiration for a gunrunner, but, personally, I would prefer Hitchin Smith to a Porton Down scientist any day.'

'I see little to distinguish one from the other,' she muttered, still blazing at Johnny's disregard for her feelings.

Sir John was silent for a moment until the fire died from her eyes. Johnny and Marieanne used each other as targets when releasing their temperaments, neuroses, and emotions. For that reason alone it could be said they needed each other.

'Smith is quite an enterprising young man,' he eventually went on. 'Was born in Lancashire thirty-four years ago, the son of a coalminer and one of nine children. Now he's almost a millionaire, and it's all gun-running money. He won't have any qualms about selling to the Arabs; he's done it before. On one occasion he salvaged much of what he'd supplied from the desert after the retreat then resold it all back to them. He spends a lot of his time in Beirut, where he has an air charter company as a sideline which is run by a rather dubious Iraqi friend of his.'

Marianne shrugged in submission. There was no point in arguing, but she would deal with Johnny later.

Sir John stood, stretched and yawned. So, he was mortal. Maybe he even slept on occasions.

'Before leaving I want you to read Smith's complete file. Then go home and have a good sleep. Armstrong will brief you later with instructions on your actual contact with Smith. Take care and remember Carlyle. I doubt if there is anyone else after your hide now you've disposed of those two, but don't take any chances. I only have four top-grade agents left now — you two, Curtis and Palmer. Replacements are as scarce as hens' teeth.'

'I'll put an ad. in the *Telegraph* later, sir,' Johnny remarked.

There had been a time, during Marieanne's marriage, when Sir John had held a dozen top-grade agents in his clutches. Then Bob had been killed; Myra Stone, the only other woman in the group, turned bad; she even became an embarrassment to the Russians and Johnny strangled her in a Berlin hotel: that had been one of his mopping-up operations. Cairo had been the graveyard of four over the past year and the likeable little queer, Paul Ferndell, who was as clever as a fox, finally met his death in New York after a highly suspect party and was found in an alley the next morning, crushed into a trash can.

* * *

Marieanne sat in the outer office at Sir John's secretary's desk. She drank count-less coffees as she read the file on Hitchin Smith. It was a fat file — as complete and detailed as only a Secret Service file could be. One thing, however, set it apart from

27

most dossiers she had read — it was interesting. Smith's colourful personality and life beamed out from the typed foolscap sheets.

Sir John had gone home and there was just herself, Johnny, and the night staff left.

She read the file from cover to cover, browsed through the photographs again, then formed a brief picture of the gunrunner in her mind.

Hitchin Smith had never learned more than an odd phrase of any foreign language. Neither had he ever owned a home or a car. He lived in hotels and service apartments, travelled by air and drove exclusively rent-a-car. His only valuable possession was the Cessna Sky-wagon he had bought for his charter partnership in Beirut.

No country was closed to him and most extended him V.I.P. welcomes. His reputation was built on fair prices and straight dealing. If the customer desired the best and could pay for it, then Smith would provide him with the latest designs and models. If the customer was struggling then the arms would be old

— possibly obsolete, but they always satisfied and repeat orders were frequent.

Women were fascinated by Smith's flamboyant handsomeness and the offbeat clothes he wore. His reputation as a lover was second to none. His affairs blended both into and in between his work and, with no difficulty, he roamed into the hearts, and beds, of many beautiful women, including the wives of Cabinet Members, a couple of Prime Ministers' wives, and one Madame President. Many of these liaisons had eased the way to a successful deal but none of them had had either depth or permanence. He roamed restlessly from one woman to another.

His first sixteen years in Lancashire had left certain attractive facets to Smith's character: although his bearing and manners slotted perfectly into any background from palace to tent, the dark satanic mills still shadowed his accent, and the bluntness and dry humour were undeniably North Country.

Marieanne shut the file and sat back.

'Very interesting, all in all.' She smiled. 'As you say — he's no fool.'

'Quite a bed-hopper as well,' Johnny remarked. 'You should have fun, love.'

He rang for the file clerk, who appeared almost immediately and whisked the folder back to hidden regions of security.

'I'm so tired I think I'm past sleep, Johnny.'

'I'll drive you home.'

She looked up and shook her head.

'Don't bother — we live in different directions — or had you forgotten?'

They left the office.

'But my flat's not been used for ages,' he protested. 'It'll be all cold and damp. Besides I could rock your cradle.'

'Sleeping tablets are more reliable; they expect nothing in return.'

'Oh, so you're keeping yourself all pure for our swinging gunrunner,' he grinned snidely. 'Don't forget to turn off this temporary wave of frigidity when you're with him. Remember — the line of duty and all that crap.'

'I thought you would have backed me up about working with him,' Marieanne said, then dashed down the stairs in front of him.

As they stepped out into the grey morning Johnny took her hand. She turned as they crossed over to their two cars and smiled faintly. His grip tightened and he rubbed his other hand over her wrist. They stopped by his white Citroën.

'Goodbye, I'll see you later, Johnny, when you come round to give me my course on how to find a gunrunner and seduce him in three easy stages.'

'One easy stage, darling. There isn't time for more so I'm afraid you'll have to settle for a crash course — with practical demonstration, of course.'

Still holding her hand, he unlocked the car door and opened it.

'I still think I should drive you home. You might fall asleep at the wheel . . . '

'During a five-minute drive?'

'You might even be set upon by big bad Arabs again,' he persisted. 'Besides, I've missed you, Marieanne.'

'Surely if the need for sex was so great you could have called one of your bed-happy girl friends.'

'Yes I know I could, darling, but I wanted *you*, so don't be such a nasty little bitch. Come on, be a devil and hop in. Take a gamble on life for once.'

She looked at him for a moment, shrugged, then pulled her hand from his and got into the car.

'And there's no need to look so bloody pleased with yourself either. You mightn't find the second round quite so easy to win.'

Johnny sat beside her and knew, only too well, the truth behind her warning. He just might finish up on the settee, or even out on his neck, if he didn't play his cards very carefully. Marieanne could be a difficult and complex person to deal with, but he understood her. He bent forward and kissed her forehead.

'Do you know my philosophy on life with you, lover?'

'Which one? There have been quite a number.'

'Oh — men may come and men may go, but I go on for ever.'

And Johnny was quite satisfied with that arrangement — for most of the time.

'At times, Johnny, your self-confidence and conceit are quite remarkable!'

He grinned and pulled the gear-change over.

'It's not so much my self-confidence and conceit as the fact that I'm irresistible.' The car rose slowly on its suspension.

'Oh my God! Let's change the subject!'

'I don't like gunrunners,' Marieanne announced as they drove out of the square.

'Maybe he's allergic to secret agents.'

'Just think of all the misery they cause throughout the world. They profit from death and destruction.'

'Oh, spare me the sermon, Marieanne, not only gunrunners profit out of war. Let's face it — both you and I have made quite a packet on the side out of some pretty sickening situations. Anyway, you'll soon get to like him: he looks a sexy sod.'

'I don't care what kind of a sod he looks.'

'And neither are you going to care what kind of a job he does when you're in bed with him. Tomorrow night you'll be lying in his arms thinking he's as handsome and wonderful as that Russian, what's 'is name. After all, he's just a salesman.'

The reference to the Russian earned him a witheringly caustic glare and he immediately regretted it. Now the odds in favour of him sharing Marieanne's bed for the rest of the night were considerably lower.

'A salesman of death, you mean,' she snapped.

2

Hitchin Smith sat at the bar, stabbing the cherry in his whisky sour and feeling alternately satisfied and dissatisfied. Satisfied because he had just made himself a great deal of money — money that was safe from the clutches of his arch-enemy, the Inland Revenue; and dissatisfied because he had been obliged to leave Portofino rather rapidly the day before, due to an unreasonably jealous husband whose private detectives were too smart for words.

He had resigned himself to a few weeks in London. Whether he would be able to stand the Hilton for that length of time was doubtful. Maybe the bird stakes would take a swing in his favour: he was on holiday and needed a woman to help him enjoy this self-inflicted and totally unremunerative interlude.

There had to be some anchorage in life and London was his instinctive choice.

His birthplace in the north had been completely discarded eighteen years before when a rusty old merchant vessel had carried him away from the grey drizzle of Manchester and the never-ending strife of an over-large and under-financed coalmining family.

For almost a year he had stayed at sea, until he realised that there was no point in substituting bad living conditions, poor food, and rough company on dry land for bad living conditions, poor food, and rough company at sea. He had to get on in life and make money — as he had spent most of his childhood informing family and friends he was going to do. He had to make a great deal of money, and the only person Hitchin Smith was prepared to work for was Hitchin Smith. He wasn't going to line anyone's pockets but his own.

Eventually, after a great deal of thought, one or two minor errors, then one mighty inspiration that came to him like a bolt from the blue, Hitchin Smith became a salesman: not the nine-to-five type of salesman who earns fifteen pounds a week plus one per cent of the takings. Smith sold guns, and he sold them in a big way.

Anyone considering rebellion, minor guerrilla tactics, wholesale war, or just a little spot of subversion here and there, could do no better than get in touch with him. There was one over-riding condition: all deals were strictly cash on the nail — either pounds sterling or dollars U.S.

Smith had no interest in causes or politics; he never became involved in his customers' affairs. What they did was none of his business.

He finished the whisky sour, ordered another, then proceeded to stab the new cherry viciously. Again he mentally applauded himself on his affluence. He glanced at the cuffs of his pale-grey silk shirt, and flicked ash from the darker grey worsted jacket that was double-breasted and fitted. He sat up, looked into the mirror behind the bar and fingered the knot of his pink Liberty print tie. He shouldn't have drunk so much; the view beyond his own reflection wasn't too clear, but clear enough to see a girl, and she was quite some bird. He closed his eyes, re-opened them, and focused hard on the image. Yes, she was really something *and* was alone and walking towards the bar. He made a quick survey of the unattached men around him: no doubt she was meeting one of them. He glanced into the mirror again; she was looking straight at him.

She sat on the vacant stool by his side and her eyes still arrested his. They were large, dark-brown eyes, set in a very beautiful face. For a few seconds he studied this girl who seemed to have dropped before him like manna from heaven — the answer to all his prayers. He marvelled at her loveliness; her very short white lace dress with the high neckline and tight, wrist-length sleeves; and her long, slim legs. Again he looked up for the man who would, at any second, sweep her away from him. But there was no one. Maybe she was early.

'Good evening, Mr Smith.' Her voice was soft.

'Good evening, beautiful girl. I'm afraid you put me at a grave disadvantage as I don't think I know you. But you're more than welcome all the same. Would you like a drink?'

'My name is Marieanne, and I would like a drink — a brandy please — neat.'

Smith ordered her drink. He'd had enough, especially now the possibility of a lively night lay ahead.

'Marieanne what?'

'Marieanne Payne.'

He held her left hand and touched the ring.

'Mrs Payne?' he whispered.

'Yes.'

'And where is Mr Payne tonight — at home minding the six brawling brats?'

Husbands were a pet hate of Smith's and the memory of a very angry and voluble Signor Picone still hung heavily in his mind.

'I really don't know,' she answered, 'but wherever he went I hope he's happy. He's dead.'

'That's fortunate for me, isn't it?' he smiled. 'Whether it is for you also I wouldn't know.'

She didn't rise to his brashness. He was

as blunt as his file had revealed and very sure of himself. She would have liked to have pulled him down a peg, but she had to play the game according to the rules — rules of State.

'And there are no brawling brats,' she added.

'I didn't think there were, but it seemed to round the question off.'

Smith handed her the brandy and pushed his cigarettes across.

'Tell me,' he went on, 'what is a lovely thing like you doing in a place like this?' He waved his hand vaguely at the room, 'And accosting strange men to boot.'

As well as a strong northern accent, he sported a rather dramatic stageyness that had obviously been affected over the years as his confidence and ego increased.

'You are no stranger to me, Mr Smith. I came here especially to see you.'

He was surveying her carefully. God, but she was bloody gorgeous! Her long dark hair — not black but the darkest brown, like rich bitter chocolate — was caught back in a white bow at the nape of her neck. Distinctive dark make-up framed the almond-shaped eyes. Her skin was peachy and the faultless features animated. She could have been no more than five-foot three.

Even the movement of her fingers on the brandy glass excited Smith and just looking at her worked through to the marrow of his bones. He knew he wanted to take her to bed. He wanted her very much; and Hitchin Smith usually got what he wanted. Signora Picone was completely forgotten.

'So I have a fan!' He smiled.

'And I have a proposition — for you,' Marieanne added.

Smith didn't speak. Beautiful women with 'propositions' worried him and his first instinct was to get up and run. Her lovely mouth was smiling at him and the dark eyes twinkled; maybe she sensed his discomfort. But what harm could listening to her proposition do, he assured himself. She was only a girl and no girl had ever harmed Hitchin Smith. Obviously she had gone to some trouble in tracing him so the least he could do was listen to her.

'Tell me of your proposition, Marieanne.'

'How would you like to make two hundred thousand pounds?'

Again he smiled.

'I already have two hundred thousand pounds.'

'I know, Mr Smith, but surely you don't intend to retire at such a young age. What I am offering is tax free and cash.'

'Tax-free cash is the only kind I deal in, girl. How many dragons would I have to slay to earn this princely sum?'

'You don't have to do anything you haven't done dozens of times: just sell some guns.'

The smile had died and her eyes pierced into his, carefully analysing his reaction. Calculated efficiency veiled her sensuality for a few seconds.

'So you know my name, what my profession is, and that I am wealthy,' he muttered. 'You are very well informed.'

'We have to be, Smith: this is the age of communication . . . '

'We?' he interrupted. 'You mean you have a sister?'

Again he poked at the cherry in the bottom of his empty glass. He impaled and lifted it; it fell on to the bartop. He looked at the barman, who had his back to them, then winked at Marieanne.

'Shall I?' he asked.

'What?'

He flicked the cherry with his finger. It shot over the bar and bounced off the rear of the barman, who spun round; but everybody was involved with themselves; talking, laughing and gazing into space. He shrugged and returned to his cocktail shaker.

'Right,' Smith smiled, 'you were going to tell me about your sister.'

Marieanne bit her lip. He wasn't taking her seriously but she had been prepared for that: his women usually had far more sexual power than brain power.

'I have no sister, Mr Smith, but I do have a boss and he has a great number of guns and other armaments to dispose of. He also has a potential customer in mind.'

'Then why not make the deal yourselves and net an extra two hundred thousand?'

'That is out of the question. My boss is an American and our customer is an Arab guerrilla leader. The American government wants peace in the Middle East and is pledged to uphold Israel's right to exist as a free nation. So my boss, who is a fairly prominent citizen, doesn't want to find himself up before a Grand Jury. And I can't do it: no self-respecting Arab would deal with a female. You are the man we need, Mr Smith. You have the connections, the knowledge and also your own means of transport.'

It was all happening at such an alarming speed; Smith lit another cigarette. He began to feel very warm.

Marieanne opened her orange handbag and slipped a small piece of paper over to him.

'Pick that up and you will discover that you are Britain's newest millionaire.'

Smith took the paper and turned it over. It was a deposit slip stub for his Swiss bank in the sum of twenty-five thousand pounds sterling: just the amount required to put his total account at a million pounds.

'It's dated today,' he said.

'Yes — deposited first thing this morning.'

'By you?'

'No.'

'By who then?'

'Does it matter?'

'Well, what's it for? It's not my birthday.'

'It's on account of the two hundred thousand.'

'Well, my God, you and your boss are getting a bit bloody ahead of yourselves, aren't you? I haven't said I'll do anything yet. Besides, I feel in need of a holiday at present. The need to become a millionaire comes second.'

'But you already are a millionaire, Mr Smith.'

'Yes I am — now. And, for Christ's sake, stop calling me Mr Smith.'

He stood, brushed ash from his suit, then sat down again. Marieanne surveyed him with round, childlike eyes.

'You and your boss, whoever he is, have sort of put me on the spot. I've got twenty-five thousand quid of his: what if I don't do the job?'

'He would expect you to return the money. However, like you, he is a very wealthy man and could stand the loss should you decide to keep it. He wouldn't be very pleased about it, though.'

'I'll bet he wouldn't!'

Early in life Smith had discovered that money never grew on trees. Easy money always had a catch — then it wasn't easy money any more.

He turned what sparse information he had over in his mind. He had dealt with Arabs before; transactions with them were no more difficult than with anyone else. In fact, the Arabs went through arms at an incredible rate; possibly because they always retreated light.

'Why has your boss sent *you* to see me?'

'He doesn't want to reveal himself, so you will never know his identity. Besides, a woman has a distinct advantage in persuading a man, don't you think?'

'Maybe so, but how do you know I'm not as camp as a Boy Scouts' jamboree?'

Marieanne smiled.

'We didn't have to do much homework to discover that you are perfectly normal, Hitchin. Also I must add that my presence throughout the deal is a condition, so you might as well get used to me straight away.'

Smith touched the corners of his moustache. He had always worked alone and told her so.

'But this is different. You are working as agent for my boss and the whole of the cash will be handed over. If you were alone it would be given to you and you could bag the lot. I shall see that nothing like that happens. Then, when everything has been completed, I shall give you your one hundred and seventy-five thousand.'

'And you will take the rest home to Daddy?'

'Exactly.'

'How much is the deal worth?'

'One million — less your cut.'

'And what about *your* cut?'

'Oh I shall be all right.'

Smith stubbed out his cigarette, leaned forward and pulled the ribbon from her hair.

'Well, my love, you are obviously a very efficient business woman: a smart-arse of the first order. When I know you better, and you prove yourself acceptable company, then I shall think about it.'

Marieanne looked at him and grinned. Then she laughed softly and shook her head. Her hair fell forward and Smith forgot all about guns and Arabs and wads of cash.

'You are very beautiful, Marieanne,' he said quietly. 'But then, I expect men frequently tell you that. You must stay close to Uncle Hitchin while he considers matters because he's greatly in need of a lovely young thing to talk to and take out and . . . '

'And?' She raised her eyebrows and they were lost under the fringe.

'Oh.' He waved his hand in the air. 'Anything, anything at all. You name it and we'll do it. But let's get out of this bloody awful mausoleum of repressed freaks and do wild things. We'll find some kinky, psychedelic cellar to writhe in for a few hours.'

He was on his feet immediately and, like a shot, whisked her out of the bar.

*   *   *

Hitchin Smith sat up in the big bed, leaned against the black silk padding of the headboard and looked down at Marieanne. Her hair spread over the pillow in tousled profusion; her face, free from make-up, was peaceful and almost childlike in sleep. He wanted to stroke the soft cheek, but feared disturbing her. One hand was clenched above her head, the other lost beneath the sheet. For a long time he continued to watch, hoping she would waken so he could hold her and retrace their earlier trips into erotic pleasure. He wanted to see the fire in her dark eyes again as he took her to the wild climax of their journey.

The night before was now a jangling and exhausting memory. They had danced for hours in a mind-blowing discothéque to a loud group and a hairy, apparently oversexed singer. A lot of brandy and whisky had been consumed and Smith was increasingly conscious of Marieanne's sexual attractiveness. Every movement of her body; her hair as she tossed it back from her face; the rise and fall of her breasts as she breathed — everything about her was seering into him and he desperately wanted to make love to her. Finally he took her hand.

'I've had enough of this bloody place. I want you to myself.'

She had laughed. Her mouth was perfect, her teeth small and very white. They left and again he sank down into the luxury of her Citroën.

Then he was in her flat and walked around it, admiring the design, decoration and furnishings while Marieanne made coffee. It was meticulously tidy and obviously expensive. On the walls were a number of abstract paintings — all riots of brilliant colour. He looked closely at them and wondered who the artist J.A. was. Johnny had, of course, moved back to his own flat earlier. The shelves contained French and English books; French newspapers and copies of *Paris Match* filled the magazine rack.

Two strong coffees and one cigarette later Smith was back at full power and ready for the kill. The offensive began with a minor skirmish on the settee followed by a hasty advance to the bedroom. They laughed as they flounced on the bed, each fumbling impatiently with the other's clothes and flinging them on to the floor.

He remembered swearing as she teasingly resisted his attempts to remove the last obstacle — a sheer nylon body stocking that managed to both cover and expose everything vital at the same time. For a moment they had struggled until, trapped by a long, hard kiss, Marieanne gave in, her hands fell to her sides and Smith slowly peeled off the offending garment. For a moment his hands and eyes discovered and explored her appetising nakedness. She was soft but firm and he was aware of her obvious physical fitness.

But his need put an early end to the preliminaries and he had made love to her — and again, and again, until every drop of alcohol had evaporated from his body. After a long peaceful silence, he made love to her once more — slowly, soberly and seriously, and this time he was deeply conscious of her uninhibited response, the warmth and tightness of her body, and the fact that it was better each time.

Then he had moved off her and lay exhausted by her side, his face pressed in the pillow. Soon they were both in a deep, contented sleep.

Now he knew the name of the potential customer Smith was sold on the arms deal. In fact, he was more than satisfied when he took Marieanne into consideration. She was guaranteed company and had already proved herself satisfactory in many ways.

He had never worked as an agent before. It meant he did not take all the profit but it was a big deal and two hundred thousand quid wasn't to be sniffed at. The main advantage was that all the hard work was out of his hands; he didn't have to shop around to buy and demonstration samples of the smaller arms would be at Beirut waiting for them. Another point in its favour was El Dashiki's dire need for arms and Marieanne's reassurances that he had more than enough money to pay for them. The disadvantages had yet to reveal themselves.

Eventually Marieanne moved; the hand on the pillow opened and the fingers outstretched stiffly for a few seconds. Her shadowy eyes flickered open.

'Good morning,' Smith greeted.

She rubbed her face then smiled.

'How come you're awake after such a hard night?'

'I don't need much sleep and, besides, only a fool would sleep with a girl like you next to him.'

'So I am pleasing you, my Master?' she teased.

'Pleasing! You're bloody marvellous! A lovely girl to be both with and in, so to speak. I'm not going to let you go in a hurry.'

'Then you will have to accept my boss's proposition, won't you? If you don't Marieanne will vanish into a puff of blue smoke, never to be seen again.'

'And that is the only way I can keep you for a while?'

'Yes.'

Marieanne ran her fingers through his thick hair. For a moment Smith looked down at her then leaned close.

'Then I accept your proposition, my love, foolish though I may be for doing so. But I want much more of you and knowing that I can have you plus two hundred thousand pounds is a terrible temptation.' He pressed his finger against her nose.

'Tell me, Hitchin, was it the money or me that finally swung you?'

'You. I don't really need the money, but I feel I need you.'

She smiled and Smith sighed.

'So you have succeeded, Marieanne. Your boss will be pleased.'

'Oh he will, Hitchin — pleased with us both. He wanted you to do this above anyone else. You are a self-made man and have come a long way from the grime of Swinton to the Hilton; and from scrubby mill girls to Signora Picone.'

Smith glanced at her then fell back against the pillows. When she said things like that he became worried again. Why had she to be such a well-informed know-all?

'Is there anything about me you don't know?'

'I don't think so. You nearly drowned in the canal at the end of your street when you were three. You were brought before the juvenile court when you were nine for blowing up a neighbour's grandfather clock. Until you left school and went to sea, you were nothing more than an insolent trouble-causer.'

'You're right, girl, you're dead right!'

'We know everything about you, Hitchin; from the day you were born until now.'

'And I know nothing of you. Dare I ask?'

She smiled.

'Try.'

There were many things he wanted to ask; like the reason for the battered tailor's dummy at the opposite end of the room. He doubted that Marieanne was a home dressmaker. The dummy was completely ruined; the chest area one gaping gash that spewed stuffing. An inspection of the cabinet at her side of the bed would have revealed two knives and an air pistol; also sheets of paper divided into columns — 'M' and 'J', with scores listed underneath.

But he was more curious about the white weals on her shoulder-blade — evidence of a dreadful beating some time in the past.

'Does your boss bash you when you don't succeed?' He touched the marks lightly.

She said not. He pressed for an explanation but all she would say was that one couldn't always be popular.

He asked about her husband. She told him he'd been killed in an air crash twelve months before.

'He must have left you well provided for. Or is this pad with the compliments of your boss?'

She laughed softly, fell back against the pillows and slid her hands behind her neck.

'This is my pad, Hitchin, not my boss's. And my husband did leave me well provided for.'

'I just wondered whether I'm in your boss's usual place.' He banged his fist down on his side of the bed.

'Wrong,' she said. 'Definitely wrong.'

'Then he isn't aware of *all* your talents?'

He wanted to know the story of her life and Marieanne knew she had to ply him with a certain amount of frankness and sincerity. If she held back he would be wary — he might even change his mind about the job.

So she told him the plain, unvarnished truth of her childhood until she was eighteen: of how she had been born nearly twenty-seven years before to a wealthy Irish industrialist and his French wife. She explained how Mama had left Father, unable to stand his adulterous affairs, and had taken Marieanne to France. Five years later Mama died and the Ledroite family hadn't wanted the responsibility of raising a young and precocious child. So Marieanne was returned, with great haste, to her father in England, who would have preferred not to have had a daughter at all.

Patrick O'Connor had brought her up to the best of his limited paternal abilities by packing her off, first to an Irish convent, then an English one. On the first day of each school holiday she was put on a plane to Paris to be looked after by Mama's family, who returned her to England just as eagerly on the last day.

In order to keep her out of his hair, her father spent a phenomenal amount of money on her education and many expensive whims. When she was older he imposed no restrictions — other than ordering her not to become pregnant.

At the point where she had left school at eighteen, with four A levels and no ambition, Marieanne let fantasy step in and finished the tale with a university education, jobs abroad and, finally, having met her present boss two years before.

Smith listened, without interrupting, then took her in his arms.

'It's time I started earning my two hundred thousand, don't you think?'

'Yes,' she agreed, 'by first of all looking after my interests — again.'

Her fingers traced lightly over his face and her body moved against his.

'Then we'll fly to the mystic and

magical east . . . '

Her words were lost as he kissed her. Then he raised his head, pressed his finger against her nose again and laughed softly.

'And then, my girl, you will have the great honour of meeting my faithful lackey, Ali Baba, the original Thief of Baghdad.'

But she wasn't listening — her eyes told him she wasn't listening. And Hitchin Smith forgot about guns, money and Ali Baba, to join her again in the completely selfish but pleasurable quest of satisfying their desires.

3

A grey, chilly drizzle had bathed London Airport on their departure; Beirut greeted them with sunbaked, humid intensity.

Marieanne waited at the side of the lounge watching Smith, who paced up and down, each lap faster and angrier than the last. Ali Baba wasn't there to meet them. Continually he brushed hair from his forehead, tucked the wide tie back inside his open jacket and gave Marieanne shrugs of irritable desperation.

Why the hell had he to crash around like that, drawing so much attention to himself, she wondered? But, of course, Hitchin Smith would see no reason for caution. He was a popular man in the Arab world. Their easy passage through Customs had proved that: officials had fallen over themselves each outdoing the other with exaggerated servility and politeness. Chalk marks were flicked on unopened baggage and they had been

M'sieured and Ma'mseilled, bowed and saluted right through the system. Only a few months before Smith had sold arms to the Lebanese Government and the authorities were obviously under the misguided impression that a repeat order was coming up.

Marianne moved farther back and sat down in the corner. Her French passport identified her as Michelle Lessard. She wore an orange crepe outfit, with loose trousers and a long, belted sleeveless jerkin. Underneath was a white blouse and many links of tiny coloured beads. Square gilt-framed glasses with amber lenses, and hair brushed back under an orange band, gave her quite a different appearance.

Police and troops outnumbered civilians. Marieanne looked around the lounge: a pall of tension and insecurity blanketed everyone. To burst a paper bag would probably have set off a major panic. But there seemed little point in this outward show of defence as, through the window, was the horse that bolted before the stable door had been shut: half the

Lebanese commercial airfleet lay dead and decaying around the airport. The wreckage had been pushed clear of the runways and left — a cold reminder of Israel's recent vicious reprisal.

Smith was on his way back from another tour of the lounge and baggage check hall. He managed to make the air-conditioning appear thoroughly inefficient by continually pulling at his collar. Marieanne cringed inwardly, visualising Israeli agents lurking in every shadow, ready to pick off one of their enemy's chief arms suppliers like a ripe jaffa in an orange grove. Long training and experience led her always to act inconspicuously.

'The bloody fool's never been so late before,' he began on reaching her. 'God, he's an impossible little bastard!'

She had heard the story of Ali Baba, Smith's lackey and partner, during the flight from London.

He had first met the wiry little Iraqi in Baghdad five years before. His parents had named him Mahommed Salah Assad, but Smith soon changed that. He was immediately intrigued by the Arab's extraordinary abilities — mainly as a thief: Ali Baba stole that which he needed, and that which he didn't need. He had even stolen his wife from a harem in Saudi Arabia. Smith soon learned the deep and burning ambitions of this smooth-tongued wheedler: he wanted enough money to buy a plane — a little plane would do, but just large enough to fly a portion of the Lebanese hashish crop into Egypt, Jordan, and Syria each year. So Smith bought the plane and Ali Baba beamed in pleasure, swore eternal loyalty to the Englishman, and assured him that they were now in a most lucrative business. Not that Hitchin Smith ever reaped the benefits of Ali Baba's enterprises: the books disclosed a terrifying loss for the partnership each year. But Ali's gold teeth continually increased in number; an addition to his already large family was an annual event, and a new helicopter eventually enlarged the company's assets. So Smith resigned himself to an investment that presented a nil dividend, and probably always would. He didn't really care: the little charter company had become invaluable to him; Ali was always on hand to fly him around and fetch and carry for him. Soon he was an integral part of Smith's gunrunning business — in and between the hashish harvest.

'Maybe he's waiting for us outside,' Marieanne suggested.

'Probably — having a kip in his car. Come on, let's go find him.'

She looked around, wondering where Johnny was: he would be there somewhere — out of sight, but watching them both. He had flown to Beirut the day after her recall to London.

Smith walked through the entrance, raised his hand against the sun and looked out.

'There he is, the lazy little wog!' He pointed vaguely towards the far side of the road. 'He's in the car, like I said. I'll soon sort him out.'

He hurried across and Marieanne followed slowly, dodging the mad traffic. It was hot and sticky — too hot to rush. Then she saw the car — a large and very long old Dodge, in anaemic sunbleached yellow, patched from top to bottom with red, green, blue and rust. Dents possibly outnumbered patches and rope fastened the boot down to the bumper bar. It was a sight never to be forgotten and she smiled.

Smith reached the car and pulled viciously at the door. He stooped, leaned inside, but the stream of abuse died at birth. Marieanne saw him stiffen. She also saw sunlight reflect on the driver's gun as Smith stood back against the open door. She stopped and cursed herself for letting him barge into the trap. She should have foreseen trouble. Maybe they were Arabs and her true identity known. Capture would ruin everything. She had to get away or finish up like Carlyle. But as she turned her path was blocked: a gun covered her from the depths of a pocket, motioning her back towards the car.

Smith was already in the back seat and Marieanne was pushed into the front. Her captor flung their cases into the boot then sat beside Smith. The car roared through Khalde towards the city.

She looked at the driver. He was a big, flabby man with the torso of an all-in wrestler. The man in the back was young. There was something vaguely un-Arab about them both and suspicions began to grow in her mind.

Smith spoke first.

'What the hell is all this about? You can't go around kidnapping tourists. It's a bloody rude way to treat people who bring good money into your country.'

Marieanne felt like applauding his act of righteous indignation. But Smith *was* indignant: trouble had never entered his mind.

'This is not our country, Mr Smith.' The driver spoke.

'Israelis might I suggest?' she offered in a soft French accent and looked from one to the other. They smiled.

'Correct, Madame.'

'Where are we being taken to?' Smith asked after a pause. He sat back, hands clasped together on his knee. The gun covering them made him reluctant to move.

'To your airstrip,' the driver replied.

'Then your man will fly us all down to Haifa.'

'What for?'

'Mr Smith, how hurt and innocent you sound!' It was the young man beside him who spoke. Strong traces of American remained in his voice. 'You say you are tourists. Both you and your business are well known to us. We also know your lady friend — and *her* business.'

Marieanne turned; the meaningful emphasis on the last three words and the look in the dark eyes told all. They knew exactly who she was and why she was with Smith. Not that it really surprised her: the Israelis were clever little bastards, with their noses and ears into everything. All she could do was pray neither of them would go into detail and blow her cover sky high. That would immediately put an end to Smith's part in the mission.

Smith realised the futility of his protested innocence.

'You can't stop people from doing business,' he argued.

There was no reply and nothing more was said, which suited Marieanne.

The car roared through heavy traffic towards the centre of Beirut then slipped into and wound through side streets and lanes until they reached the north-east corner of the city. They crossed the bridge towards Jdaidé and the metropolis slipped back as they headed north along the coast road.

Marieanne felt the first panic of desperation stabbing her: was Smith just going to sit there and let them both be flown into Israel? Again this proved the folly of working with an amateur. There would be none of the co-ordination of thought and action that occurred automatically when she worked with Johnny. All Smith did was sit and complain.

Her thoughts were fragmented as the car squealed round a sharp bend; Smith suddenly raised himself and leaned across the seat. A gust of wind poured in; Marieanne turned and saw the young Israeli spinning and bobbing along the side of the road behind them. The driver began to shout.

'You Arab-loving pigs!' he roared in Hebrew and swung the car to the left into a side road. He drove wildly until they came to a narrow track then turned into it, pumping the brake. The car screeched and swerved as he tried to take the gun from his jacket. The far side of the track was a sheer drop to the sea.

Marieanne grabbed his upper arm, her fingers digging deep into the nerve points until the gun dropped to the floor. Her other hand pulled at the steering wheel; she swung the car away from the edge and they came to a spinning halt.

Smith threw himself over the front seat. Both he and the driver tumbled out on to the ground.

They struggled to their feet and tore into one another like tigers, but Smith's punches made little impression in the mass of muscle and fat. The Israeli lashed out with the ease of a professional.

Marieanne picked up the gun and joined them on the track. She sat on the bonnet of the car and watched, the gun resting on her knee. She didn't want to interfere in the fight unless absolutely necessary; there was too much danger of hitting the wrong target.

Smith was a good fighter, but sheer size and weight was against him. The Israeli smashed viciously at his head and he fell back against a high heap of boulders. He didn't move and his arms fell limply to his side.

The Jew moved in to deliver the final blow. Marieanne tensed when she saw just how close they were to the edge. Her fingers closed tight on the trigger and she aimed. He was ready to strike and she was ready to fire. But Smith suddenly kicked out and both feet smashed into the bloated stomach. With a dull cry the Israeli folded like a penknife. He staggered backwards. For a second his feet tottered along the cliff edge, little stones shuffling under his weight and scattering backwards. Then he stepped back farther and fell, screaming, into the void towards the rocks and the sea far below.

Smith looked down. The body had caught against a small outlet of rock and hung from it precariously. Then its weight dislodged the rocks and they fell, with the body, to the bottom in a cloud of dust. Smith didn't like what he saw; he didn't like what he'd done. He turned and walked back to Marieanne, wiping blood from the corner of his mouth. She was still sitting on the bonnet but the gun was underneath her bag.

'You're supposed to straighten your jacket now,' she said. 'Brush the dirt off it and tuck your shirt in: that's what they do in films.'

'All right, smart-arse, a fat lot of help you were. That pig was at least five stones heavier than me and all you did was sit there like a floozy at a prize fight.'

'I had his gun.' She waved it in front of him.

'I bet you don't know one end of a gun from the other.'

'Oh yes I do.'

'Well then, why the bloody hell didn't you use it?'

'Because you were too close together. I might have shot you by mistake. Besides, I wanted to see how you handle yourself in a fight.'

'Oh now that's really lovely! I hope I didn't disappoint you and you enjoyed the show.'

'You didn't disappoint me, Hitchin. In fact, I'm extremely impressed with you — in quite a number of ways.'

Her eyes smiled. He took the gun from her.

'Better let me have that, before we have a nasty accident.'

She had shown no concern or distress at what had happened. The hysterical tears and need for consolation he had expected just never happened. Smith had never met such a strange girl before and, for a moment, he just looked at her.

'Let's get to the airstrip,' he finally muttered. 'God knows what kind of a state Ali's in.'

★　★　★

The airstrip, which lay to the south of Jdaidé, was a sorrowful and neglected place. Most of the buildings were crumbling or had been partially torn down, and the car no longer seemed an incongruous heap in such downtrodden surroundings.

'Look, there's our plane,' Smith pointed.

Throughout the drive Marieanne had been haunted with harrowing fears that the plane would be in a similar state to that of the car. But the Cessna stood, proud and perfect, the proverbial rose in a bed of thorns, and the sunlight exaggerated the brilliant white and red bodywork.

'I like her,' she said in relief. 'She's very attractive!'

'All my ladies are attractive. You like her: I like her: Ali Baba loves her.'

He drove the car on to a tarmac square that fronted a block of sheds. This was the nerve centre of the partnership and Ali's own private enterprises. An uninspiring sign topped the door: 'Mid-East Charter Craft Co.,' it stated, then repeated itself underneath in Arabic squiggles.

'Stay here, Marieanne.'

He got out of the car, walked slowly over to the shed, then hesitated for a few seconds at the door before pushing it open. He stepped inside out of view. Marieanne expected him to reappear almost immediately, but he didn't. Thirty more seconds, she told herself, then I'm going in.

The need for extreme caution had never really entered Smith's head, even after the fracas on the way, and he was completely staggered to find himself covered by the gun of a tall, slim individual dressed in a dark-blue shirt and jeans.

Ali Baba lay bound and gagged in the far corner.

The Israeli stared questioningly at Smith then glanced towards the door.

'What has happened? Where are the others?' He was older than the other two, and a snap of superiority edged his voice.

'One of them, at least, has died for the cause,' Smith replied.

There was an awkward pause. The Israeli's plans had gone drastically askew and he was busy reshuffling his thoughts. Ali Baba squirmed and made stupid noises through the gag.

'Where is the girl?'

Then Marieanne appeared in the doorway.

'Here I am,' she answered innocently. She had taken her jerkin off and it covered her folded arms. She looked blankly at Smith and the Israeli, then pushed the door shut with her foot.

'Move over to him,' the Jew ordered.

She shrugged and sauntered slowly across the room. Smith watched her, even more amazed at her calmness and apparent lack of fear.

'Raise your arms above . . . ' One dull phut ended the order. The Israeli's gun dropped to the floor. His hands covered his face and bright rivulets of blood flowed down through rigid fingers. He fell, face down, beside his weapon.

Marieanne took her gun from beneath the jerkin, unclipped the silencer and put them into her shoulder bag.

'You were wrong, Hitchin, I do know one end of a gun from the other.'

Smith said nothing but his knees suddenly felt like hot jelly. The whole thing had been so premeditated and perfect. The ease with which she carried it off, and the calculated look in her eyes, worried him. Then he remembered her action in the car to prevent the driver drawing his gun. At that moment a lot of things worried him and he badly needed a stiff drink.

'Don't you think you should untie your faithful lackey?' she suggested. 'I think he wants to say something.'

Smith cut Ali Baba free and she looked down at him. He stood, brushed his grubby white overalls, then pressed the thick mass of hair against his head.

'He said you had been taken at the airport and that you would be brought here.' His words came out in a rush. It was obvious Smith was his English teacher as the Middle-Eastern accent was amusingly linked with North Country vowel sounds.

'We dropped them off on the way,' Smith said.

Then Ali Baba turned to Marieanne and a big smile spread across his thin, leathery features, exposing a mouthful of gold teeth. His bright black eyes shone with pleasure. He was slight in build but sinewy. His plimsolled feet were never still; they shuffled lightly on the dusty floor like a boxer's feet. Again he wiped his hands down his overalls and extended one to Marieanne. He looked to be in his late thirties.

'You are the lady Mr Smith told me about on the phone. I know because he said you were bloody smashing, and you are.'

He shook her hand vigorously.

'Very pleased to meet you, Ma'mseille.'

She smiled and replied in French, saying she had heard a great deal about him and was, likewise, extremely pleased to make his acquaintance. He muttered modest protestations back in French, and held on to her hand.

Smith moved over and pulled Ali's hand away.

'Just keep your thieving mitts off her,' he warned. 'And speak English, both of you. I like to know what's going on. I wouldn't trust *you* farther than I could kick you, oh lustful son of the desert. Your mind needs a good decarbonising.'

'Mr Smith, how could you say such a thing? Would I rob you of your woman? Would I rob you of anything?' His eyes pleaded hurt innocence but he obviously enjoyed Smith's tormenting censures.

'Yes you would — you've been robbing me blind for years, you light-fingered bastard!'

Ali Baba shrugged a grin at Marieanne.

'He is a hard master, doubting even the good name of my parents. Ma'mseille, you are completely safe with me.'

But Marieanne was inclined to agree with Smith's sentiments: Ali Baba was ogling her hungrily with furtive sidelong glances. She liked him instinctively.

She walked to the window and looked over the scruffy airfield. The sun was high and the squeaky fan that waved slowly from side to side on top of the filing cabinet did little to dispel the heat.

'Anything been delivered?' Smith asked.

'Three boxes came yesterday. They're in the big store shed. *He* wanted to know why you were here again. I said you were on holiday, like you told me to say, but he said I was a liar and that he'd soon find out. Filthy Jewish dog!'

He kicked the body with his wrecked plimsolls.

'What will we do with him?' he went on.

Marieanne crossed back and knelt by the corpse. She turned it over and went through the pockets. They contained only Lebanese money, cigarettes, and a handkerchief.

'My God, you've made a mess of his face,' Smith commented.

The bullet had struck the forehead between the eyes. She took a wad of Kleenex from her bag and wiped the blood from the floor. Then she covered the face with more tissues but the blood soaked through.

Under the Jew's shirt was a holster. Marieanne unfastened it and put the gun back.

'Put this on, Hitchin, you may need it soon.' She threw the holster but he put it down on the table.

'Not bloody likely. I've never worn a gun.'

'Maybe you've never had trouble like this before. Wear it.'

He looked down at her. Again there was that hard, steely look in her eyes and her voice was sharp. After a moment of broody silence he took his jacket off, changed into a green paisley shirt Ali had taken from the cupboard, then made a big scene of putting on the holster.

'What will we do with *him*?' Ali repeated.

'Oh for Christ's sake have him for dinner, if you want,' Smith shouted, annoyed at having capitulated so easily to a woman.

'I'm sure Ali's conscience would object to Jew for dinner,' Marieanne smiled. 'We'll throw him out of the plane.'

'Charming! You just seem to take it all for granted. I have to eject one bloke from a car; kick another over a cliff, then you shoot this one like you do it every day. In all the years I've been running guns I've never had anything like this happen to me. Why, in heaven's name, should the Israelis be so interested in *me* all of a sudden?'

'Oh don't be so naïve. You mightn't have been troubled before, but the situation is far more acute now. The Jews know you are a gunrunner and don't want you supplying their enemy any more — which, obviously, they assume you have come here to do. They're after your hide, Hitchen.'

'And you,' Smith reminded. 'It would seem they weren't taken in by your passport and, if I may say so, rather weak attempt at disguise. The Jews have always known what I am: however, they've never bothered me before, despite the fact that both me and my business are based in Beirut — until *you* join me; then bang! Trouble from the word go. It's you they don't like girl.'

'El Sitt is brave and beautiful,' Ali chipped in. 'She is better than Barbarella.'

Smith turned and sighed at the look on Ali's face. He knew that expression: Ali Baba's admiration of and devotion to Marieanne would know no limits. 'El Sitt' (the lady) would be able to do no wrong or say no wrong and she would have to be considered and consulted before any action taken. Within fifteen minutes she had shot to the very pinnacle of the little Iraqi's popularity poll, toppling even his adored cartoon strip heroine.

Still grinning at her reverently, Ali backed out of the office, returning with their baggage.

Smith wasn't happy about the situation and already regretted accepting the job. He could manage very well and not touch the Middle East again: the new African States alone would keep his pockets well lined for years.

He walked over to the greasy, spotted mirror by the door and combed his hair. Through the glass he watched Marieanne as she stared blankly out of the window. What her thoughts and her feelings were about the events of the day intrigued him and he realised how little he knew about her. All the love, warmth and laughter they had shared had taught him nothing and the earlier impressions and conclusions he had drawn about her were smashed.

Marieanne turned. She knew what was troubling him and smiled to herself. His illusion of the helpless little woman had crumbled; his manhood was in peril, if not actually desecrated. Most men reacted that way. They weren't all like

Johnny, or her husband, or . . . For a moment her memory skipped swiftly back over her years in the Service and other men who had entered her life briefly.

'I think,' she said, 'to coin a phrase, I'll change into something more comfortable: something more in keeping with our prospective client's way of life.'

Smith pointed towards the other door:

'In there if you don't mind. We don't want Ali getting himself into a high state of frustration before the flight. It affects his navigation and we just might end up in Haifa after all.'

Marieanne changed and took stock of the situation in the seclusion of the other dusty office. The assignment wasn't even off the ground and they had been faced with unexpected opposition — the Israelis. A two-edged sword hung above them by a very ragged thread.

Smith walked in.

Her hair was tied back in a black clip, the fringe had reappeared, and she wore black jeans, sneakers and a yellow tee-shirt. She turned, slipping on her holster, and Smith admired the slight, streamlined body that complemented the boyish clothes so perfectly.

'Maybe we should get Ali to carry a gun as well,' he suggested. 'Then we'd all three match.'

'Ali can wear a feathered head-dress and carry a tomahawk for all I care.' She picked up the black denim jacket and swung it from her finger by the loop.

She wore little make-up but her beauty and youthfulness still played havoc with Smith's senses, confusing his previous ideas on women.

'I've never come across a woman like you before,' he muttered. 'You're tough and too bloody capable for words.'

'Is that cause for complaint?'

'Well, it's not very good for a man's ego. If it weren't for the fact that I've bedded you, I'd think you were completely without feelings and emotions of any kind.'

'Maybe I channel my emotions for one purpose,' she suggested.

'Maybe so.' Smith surveyed her carefully. 'You kill without feeling and think only of your own skin. Don't think I didn't see you start to run for it outside the airport. The mind positively boggles at the thought of your full potential.'

'I wouldn't have been much use to either of us had I collapsed in womanly hysteria, Hitchin. I act according to the situation. I have to — otherwise I wouldn't be here today.'

Smith shrugged.

'I don't know what kind of an outfit your boss runs, but he certainly has an extremely reliable and efficient employee in you. He must have trained you well.'

'Oh he certainly did.'

'I only hope he pays you well.'

'He does.'

She smiled and put the jacket on. Her nose and the corners of her big, brown eyes crinkled when she smiled and the efficiency and strength melted away. Smith stepped over to her. He held her shoulders and her fingers ran lightly over the moustache and across his cheeks. She kissed him and congratulated herself on having been thrust into the arms of this very attractive and likeable man.

Then all Smith could think of was that

it seemed an eternity since he had last made love to her.

'I hope these bloody freedom fighters have got decent sleeping accommodation.'

'Communal, I expect,' she teased. 'They go in for that a lot in this part of the world, don't they?'

'They better hadn't. Tonight I want comfort and four thick, soundproof walls dividing us from the rest of the world.'

He pulled her close and their mouths met hungrily.

Ali Baba knocked softly, after he had entered. For a second or two he surveyed Western passion, grinned, then tapped his partner on the shoulder. Smith jolted round in surprise.

'Jesus, but you're a sneaky little crow! Your sense of timing is way, way out!'

The Iraqi ignored the abuse.

'I've taken the cases from the store, Mr Smith. I think we should get them on board and leave right away. The radio says riots have broken out in the city again. Last week there was bad trouble and the gendarmes came here and searched everything.'

Smith released Marieanne, quietly calling on God to pity him for having to tolerate such an idiot.

⋆   ⋆   ⋆

He insisted on prising open the three cases and inspecting the samples before they took off. This delay caused Ali Baba great concern and his ragged plimsolls swished nervously back and forth over the sandy ground.

'Hey, these aren't bad at all,' Smith commented. 'Better than those bloody wogs deserve. At the first sign of attack they'll drop them, take to their heels, and the Jews'll grab the lot.'

Marieanne inspected the plane while Smith and Ali carted the cases on to the tarmac. The Iraqi was overcome by her obvious interest and admiration, and gave a long description of his precious Cessna: she was a TU 206B Turbo-System Super Skywagon, he announced proudly, with a 285 h.p. turbo super-charged engine. Under her fuselage could be fitted a cargo pack capable of holding three hundred pounds. The optional extra came into its own when the hashish harvest was on the market. There was seating for the pilot and three passengers.

The plane gleamed both inside and out and reflected the tender loving care Ali lavished on her.

The cases were loaded with the aid of a small and very old fork-lift truck which Ali drove with impatient viciousness. Then he loaded the rest of their gear and shut the side cargo doors. Only the corpse remained. He refused to touch a dead Jew so Smith dumped it on board beside Marieanne in the rear passenger seats.

After all his earlier pleas for them to leave right away, Ali decided on a last-minute engine check. Marieanne moved up to the pilot's seat and switched the radio on. She cut into a news bulletin in French: refugees were rioting in the city; a cinema was blazing, and two people had been killed. Similar demonstrations were taking place in Sidon. She translated for Smith, who sat next to her polishing his sunglasses, peering out through them, then repolishing them.

'Any trouble in Sour?' he asked. The sun blazed in through the cockpit; they had both taken their jackets off.

'Doesn't say. We seem to have chosen a bad time.'

She turned the radio off and went back to her own seat.

'You can say that again,' he flung. 'I can tell you, girl, I'm none too happy about this job. Any more trouble and this bloke's bowing out while he's still in one piece.'

Marieanne looked up at him.

'You agreed to the deal, Hitchin. Where are your business ethics?'

'They'll be dropped, just like old Isaac Rosenbloomenberger here is going to be dropped. I don't want to die yet, Marieanne. Strange as it may seem to you, gun battles, fights, and playing the big hero make me feel weak at the knees.'

Ali climbed in through the pilot's door.

'Right we are then,' he stated in his quaint Baghdad-Manchester accent, and wiped his hands on a grubby rag. 'Just wanted to make sure those Jewish dogs hadn't touched her.'

He stared at them.

'Why do you wear guns?'

'Because your precious El Sitt believes in us being prepared for trouble,' Smith replied.

'Maybe she is wise, Mr Smith. There has been much trouble already for us today and the whole country is in a mess. It is as well you come now as the Army is trying to throw all the terrorist groups out of Lebanon. Soon El Dashiki also will have to go.'

Ali sniffed, looked around, then smiled lasciviously at Marieanne and asked if she was quite comfortable. Then he ordered safety belts to be fastened in an authoritative voice and sat at the controls, flicking knobs and turning keys with great drama. Marieanne strapped the corpse in.

* * *

Ali wasn't too happy about the flight. The deserted airstrip they were heading for lay half way between Sour and Bent Jebail in the south and was too close to Israel for his comfort. He feared for the safety of his beloved plane first, himself second, and El Sitt third: Smith just didn't enter into his anxieties.

'If a day raid starts we could get shelled,' he continually complained, together with moans about the plane being overloaded.

Marieanne was silent, engrossed with sights she had never seen before. Three days in Beirut and many encounters with the airport had been her only previous experiences of Lebanon.

Ali followed the route of the Damascus Road until they were over the Lebanon mountains, then swung south, widely skirting the winter ski resorts. She followed the route on his greasy old map.

'I'm going to take her down as low as I can,' he stated, 'then she will be safe from Israeli reconnaisance.'

Marieanne peered down to select her spot and, as they topped a group of cedars, she stood. The Lake of Qaraaoun stretched out beneath them.

'Say bye bye to our friend,' she called. 'He's leaving us now.'

Smith turned. The corpse had gone and Marieanne slammed the cargo doors in the floor. He looked down through the cockpit to see the body dropping limply towards the water. He twisted round again. Marieanne was back in her seat, lighting a cigarette. She smiled at him vaguely.

Ali continued to complain as the flight proceeded: the border with Syria would soon become the border with Israel. He swung the plane due west, towards Sour, and took her higher.

'Look to your left, Ma'mseille; there is the Sea of Galilee.'

For a moment Marieanne could see where the River Jordan swelled into a pear-shaped sea not far inside Israeli territory. But it faded quickly as Ali raced the Cessna on.

Smith had told her Ali's landings were as gentle as caresses. Having decided he was a good pilot, Marieanne awaited the event with optimism. She wasn't disappointed; the plane came to a halt smoothly, with no bounce or jolt.

Then the three of them stood by the plane and looked around. All that remained of the airstrip was a sandy, scrubby runway and four crumbling walls that had once been a building.

An hour later the sun was low — almost as low as Smith's spirits. He paced up and down, as he had done at Beirut, cutting an incongruous figure against the background of wild, deserted countryside. The wind tugged at his expensive, stylish suit, flapping the flared bottoms of the trousers against his ankles. His long, unruly hair blew about in abandon. Then he turned to Marieanne, his wild eyes impatient and demanding.

'Well then, girl, where's the brass band and the welcoming committee of jolly Arab Freedom Fighters?'

4

The afternoon sauntered lazily into evening. Marieanne, Smith, and Ali Baba were still alone and wearily trod the dusty, eroded strip. Finally hunger forced a decision and Ali was sent to the nearest village for food. He ambled off in his own unique slithering fashion, kicking stones and calling on Allah to save him from such menial tasks and a hard master. Marieanne felt sorry for him as the nearest homestead must have been miles away. So she called after him that she was desperately hungry and would never forget him if he brought her something special to eat. That did the trick; Ali's unwilling shuffle turned to a trot and his prayers of despair became a happy whistle.

He returned, nearly two hours later, on a bicycle, the origins of which were never disclosed. He had enough food and drink for a feast. Smith railed him with abuse for taking so long, despite the obvious distance he had covered.

There still had been no sign of their customer's envoys. If it hadn't been for her implicit faith in Johnny's plans and arrangements, Marieanne would have been as dubious as Smith was about the whole situation.

'It's a bloody farce,' he eventually muttered, and brought the water carrier and mugs from the plane. Marieanne ignored his comments.

They lit a fire and cooked lamb and chicken on a spit, sprinkling it liberally with herbs and crushed garlic. Onions, mint, and crushed wheat grain were cooked in a tin found in the plane. Yoghurt and an enormous amount of fresh fruit served as dessert.

While they ate Smith drink arak and water. He offered some to Marieanne; she took one sip, screwed her face up and refused more. Ali, true to his faith, didn't drink. After the meal he shuffled up to Marieanne and pressed a package into her hand.

'Special for you from Ali Baba,' he whispered.

It was a large block of chocolate-covered halva which she divided amongst them. Ali squirmed in pleasure as she thanked him and complimented him on his thoughtfulness.

Smith had changed and wore jeans, a red tee-shirt, and suede jacket. He lay with his head on Marieanne's knees, hoping the arak would make him forget his depression. It did until Ali had to remind him of the time.

'It's eleven o'clock. They'll never come now,' he wailed. That preceded another long session of complaints and declarations of lack of faith by them both. Smith announced that he'd definitely had enough of the whole affair. He was for going back to Beirut there and then but, eventually, Marieanne managed to persuade him to say no more until next morning. She brought three blankets from the plane to shield them from the cold night air and settled down beside him on the softer ground at the side of the runway.

'If they haven't come by daybreak we're going back,' was his parting shot.

Marieanne nodded in agreement and stared up at the stars. Ali lay about six yards from them quietly singing weird and ghostly Arab melodies. Finally he sang himself to sleep.

Smith was rather drunk and drowsy. He held Marieanne close and she ran her fingers lightly through his hair. He made one valiant attempt at seduction that didn't get past first base: a few heady kisses; muttered endearments; a struggle with unyielding buttons and clothes, and the arak triumphed. He fell back without a care in the world and drifted into a deep sleep.

The moon was large and high, casting a cold, anaemic light on the landscape. For a while Marieanne sat carefully considering their situation. She knew Smith wasn't going to take any more and understood his feelings. But they couldn't go back: El Dashiki had to be found and approached.

She stood up, kicked earth on to the red embers of the fire, then walked over to the plane.

An hour later she was still awake,

sitting against a parachute pack about five yards from Smith. She had taken Ali's sheepskin jacket from the plane and pulled it over her shoulders. Round her head she had tied a scarf and her legs were covered with the blanket.

Then she heard voices. Her first thought was to waken the others, but as they came closer she hesitated, and a cold tingle of danger settled on the back of her neck. At first it was pure intuition that brought her to her feet and she held the Belgian assault rifle taken from the samples. Then the voices were clearer. They were coarse, drunken voices: hardly those of freedom fighters. She fell to her knees, pulled off the jacket, rolled it tightly, then pushed it under the blanket which she straightened feverishly. She glanced around, pounced on the large paper bag filled with other paper bags and scraps from the meal that they had forgotten to burn, and wrapped her scarf round it. She pushed it under the top of the blanket, against the jacket, then crept towards the crumbling building. The moonlight brightened in her imagination and the shelter of the walls seemed so far away. Finally she reached them and crouched in the shadow.

Smith and Ali were still asleep and the third blanket gave a convincing picture of another person.

Now the visitors were close to the airstrip and visible. There were three of them, on donkeys. Their voices were lowered; they had obviously seen the plane and its sleeping crew.

Marieanne climbed over the remains of a window sill and knelt behind the wall, shivering against the cold. The riders dismounted, their three rifles at the ready, and walked towards the sleepers. The barrel of her rifle rested on the sill and she took aim.

A loud hail of Arabic ordered Smith and Ali awake. They sat up slowly to find rifles against their heads. A quick hand pulled the revolver from Smith's holster.

He asked the inevitable question.
'What the hell's going on?'

Ali exchanged a barrage of words with the three intruders and, although his knowledge of Arabic was almost non-existent, Smith understood enough to know they were going to be well and truly robbed.

'They'll kill us if we don't let them have what they want,' Ali explained, his eyes wide and white with terror.

'Are you sure they haven't just come for the bicycle you stole?' Smith suggested.

'No, these aren't villagers; they're outlaws from the hills.'

Two of them walked over to the dead fire and started to sort through the objects on the ground. Then they saw Smith's radio and the bicycle, put their rifles down, and called the third man. But he refused to leave Smith and Ali and, within a few seconds, they were quibbling over possession of the two items. Smith knew it was only a matter of time before they began to plunder the plane.

In the sudden surprise of the situation he had given no thought to Marieanne. He turned to the other blanket. She was still asleep. How could anyone sleep with all this racket going on, he wondered?

The third Lebanese followed his gaze and crossed drunkenly to the huddled body. He shouted an order and exchanged more words with Ali, who crawled over to him and became very excited, waving his hands in desperation. But all he did was earn himself a kick in the chest. The other two still squabbled over their loot like children.

Smith watched the man with the rifle, who staggered back, still shouting angrily.

'He'll kill her if she doesn't wake up, Mr Smith!'

'Like hell he will!' Smith sprang forward, shouting Marieanne's name, but the outlaw swung his rifle round, smashing him across the neck. He fell back against the ground, stunned. As the bright red and yellow flashes cleared from his vision he saw the rifle point down at the motionless body. Two bullets ripped into it and the blanket twitched. Again Smith darted towards the outlaw. The rifle turned back to him and he tensed against the anticipated bullet as the barrel pressed painfully over his heart, forcing him back. But there was no bullet. Nausea gripped him; it was too late to do anything. The dirty, greasy face leered down at him and the Lebanese roared with laughter, staggering back towards his two companions.

Smith rose to his feet. If he moved quickly he might be able to get one of the rifles as the brigand's aim at a moving target wasn't likely to be good. But, before he moved, two powerful shots cracked out like a circus whip. The Lebanese leapt back, his gun dropped to the ground. He clutched his chest and stomach then fell to the ground, uttering a short strangled cry. The quarrel ceased immediately.

One of the other two outlaws grabbed his rifle and aimed at the ruined building. He fired, was answered by another shot, then slumped over the radio he had quarrelled so covetously for. The donkeys brayed in terror and took to their heels.

The third man was cut down as he ran after the donkeys. Screaming, he twisted round, both hands covering the back of his head. For a moment he writhed on the ground still screaming. Then he was still.

Smith was about to pull the blanket from his murdered girl when he heard footsteps scatter across the stones then pad across the softer ground. Ali crouched beside him, wailing in Arab torment at the cruel murder of the lovely lady. They both turned, keen to know who had despatched the three Lebanese so efficiently. Marieanne was crossing over to them, rifle in hand. She knelt beside Smith, who pulled her to him and kissed her wildly over the face and neck.

'I thought you were dead, girl, I really did.' His hands pressed into her back, forcing her to him. Ali's chatter of relief was ignored.

'He murdered me in cold blood, Hitchin: I wasn't going to stand for that.'

'No, darling, I should have known you wouldn't.'

She smiled up at him and dropped the rifle. Then her arms wrapped round his neck. From under the masculine denim Smith could feel warmth, softness and woman — and that was all he wanted.

'Now I'd like to get some sleep,' she whispered.

Smith looked up at Ali who stared at them, nodding his head and grinning.

'Well, don't just stand there gawking, you fool! Go away and get to sleep!'

Ali shuffled off and dragged his blanket a few yards nearer the plane. Muttering his usual complaints, he lay down, wrapped himself in it, and turned his back to them.

★ ★ ★

At daybreak Smith shook Marieanne awake. She lifted her head from his shoulder and knew immediately what he was going to say.

'We're going back, Marieanne.'

'What about your two hundred thousand pounds, and my boss's profit?' She sat up.

'Sod my two hundred thousand quid, darling, *and* your boss's profits. If we stay here one more day we'll all be dead.'

'But you can't go back.'

'Oh yes I can. You can have the twenty-five thousand back as soon as we get to London.'

'That isn't the point, Hitchin. We have to carry on.'

'Oh no we don't, lover. I don't care what I said I'd do in London, but I certainly didn't bargain for all this killing and trouble. I'm buggered if I'm going to risk certain death for the sake of one more job. And, another thing, if you'll take my advice you'll complain to your union, or, better still, hand in your notice when we get back. You're in too dangerous a profession for a girl. What else does your boss do besides sell arms — run a training school for homicidal maniacs?'

She said nothing. Smith looked at her and shrugged.

'Why in God's name can't you be like other girls? Get married and have babies or something.'

'We're going to carry on,' she snapped.

Ali crept up to them. He was loath to disagree with this vision of female loveliness — especially when she was such a crack shot — but there *was* the question of *his* safety involved.

'I think we should go back, Ma'mseille.'

She turned to him, her face set in anger.

'Mr Smith is being paid handsomely

for his services, Ali, and maybe you will be rewarded as well — *if* we carry on and sell the arms.'

Now Ali Baba was a very greedy fellow. The chance of even a minute portion of two hundred thousand pounds was extremely tempting. It conjured up visions of purchasing another plane; of taking on another pilot. But Ali Baba also liked to view danger from a distance — a very great distance. The closest to trouble he was prepared to go was Customs-dodging with his exportation of hashish.

So, at that precise moment, he was a very confused man.

'I don't know,' he hesitated. 'There is much money to be made and that is good. But I also want to live and see my grandchildren.'

'We're going back, Ali,' Smith stated, 'or, by this time tomorrow, the flesh will be rotting from your wretched bones.'

Smith stood and Ali followed suit.

'Yes, we go back, Mr Smith. It will be better.'

Marieanne was silent for a while. She lit a cigarette and watched as Ali began to pack the gear into the plane and Smith made a quick survey of the bodies out of curiosity. The donkeys were lost for all time.

Smith turned to her.

'Well, come on — shift yourself. We'd better move these bodies off the strip.'

'I'm not going with you,' she announced. 'So you can just unload the samples before you leave.'

That started a very dramatic argument: Smith swore and roared and threatened to put her over his knee. Ali umpired, still unable to take any one side except that of his own safety. Finally Smith reached the end of his patience and grabbed her, shaking her violently.

'You'll bloody well come back with us, Marieanne!'

'I will not!'

For a few seconds he said nothing, his anger mounting as her eyes blazed defiance at him.

'Right, you stubborn little bitch, if you won't come willingly, I'll carry you and tie you up.'

Then Ali was witness to rather a sad

incident for his partner: Smith was about to pick Marieanne up when something went drastically wrong; he somersaulted once, landing on his back. Dust rose up around him.

Marieanne smiled at Ali's amazed expression.

'And you'll get the same if you try anything,' she threatened.

Smith picked himself up and rubbed the back of his head and shoulders.

'I take it you're staying then?' he muttered.

'Yes.'

He waved his hands in submission.

'All right, stay then, with all your bloody guns, you stupid fool.'

They unloaded the sample cases and Marieanne sat cross-legged on the ground, her battered Lufthansa bag, the only luggage she had brought from Beirut, on the ground in front of her.

The plane wouldn't start. At first Ali calmly tried and retried the engine. Then impatience took over and he jumped to the ground, cursing volubly in Arabic. Smith joined him and they conferred for a moment then peered into the engine.

'Having trouble?'

They ignored her gloating question. Ali could find no reason for the engine's failure and he and Smith argued, both waving their arms and shouting, each accusing the other of negligence. They were so engrossed they didn't see the cloud of dust in the distance that was swiftly closing in on them. Marieanne stood and Smith walked over to her.

'Won't it go?' she asked.

'No, it won't bloody well go! And if you'd stop sitting there like a smirking buddha and take some interest in the proceedings, you might be able to help.'

She looked at him calmly. The light breeze blew hair across her face. She shook her head and tossed it back.

'Why should I — I'm not going anywhere. Besides, I don't know anything about planes.'

'I might have believed that a few days ago. Now I wouldn't be surprised to hear you'd been chosen to pilot the bloody Concorde.'

She smiled and screwed her face up against the sun.

'Did those devils mess with the plane before they woke us up?' he asked.

'No, they didn't go near it.' She looked beyond him and pointed. 'Look.'

Two Jeeps were within earshot and sped over to them.

Smith turned and they watched in silence. Ali took his head out of the engine and walked over to them.

The Jeeps squealed to a dusty halt. Two men jumped down wearing crisp, green drill uniforms and new black, rubber-soled boots. Their gunbelts gleamed but the rifles they held, Smith noticed, were of an obsolete and notoriously malfunctioning model.

'Mr Smith?' The elder of the two men stepped forward and saluted.

'Yes. Who are you?' He trusted no one at that stage.

'We are to escort you to our leader, El Dashiki.'

Smith said nothing; Marieanne turned to him.

'Still going back?' she whispered.

'We must apologise for being so late,' the guerrilla continued. 'Unfortunately we could not leave our caves earlier as Lebanese troops were on night patrols close by.'

After a short exchange of questions and answers they were satisfied.

Most of El Dashiki's men were Syrians, as were these two. The elder one, at first, was hostile towards Marieanne and demanded to know why a woman was involved. Smith explained that she was an essential member of the operation. The guerrilla shrugged but still refused to return her smile. The younger Syrian said little, but stared at her, periodically winking and grinning.

The samples were loaded on to the Jeeps and Ali was told to repair the plane while they were away. The talkative Syrian forgot his prejudice when Marieanne began to ply him with questions, again in the French accent she had used in Beirut, and proudly told her of El Dashiki's great wealth, well hidden caves, and his many men. A red light flashed in her mind at the mention of great wealth. She understood he was well able to pay for the arms; maybe there was far more money than the Department had estimated. She and Johnny were great believers in dipping in the till whenever safely possible — the fruits of this remunerative hobby were deposited in a Swiss bank. If they lived long enough, retirement was a pleasant prospect. Unfortunately her husband, who had amassed a small fortune, had been denied his.

Not trusting the younger guerrilla's constant eye- and teeth-flashing overtures to Marieanne, Smith climbed up beside him, leaving her to ride in the other Jeep. He was happy again and, like Marieanne, was conjuring up visions of an inflated bank account.

Ali stood by the Cessna, hands in pockets, eyes screwed up against the sun, and nodding his head slowly from side to side. He watched the Jeep until it was out of sight, leaving only a haze of smoke along the rough road.

5

Yasir Abu-Hashi sat in his office, stirred a battered mug of coffee noisily and smiled to himself. Now he foresaw an early end to two years as freedom fighter, suffering constant defeat by the Jews. When Israel surrendered the Arab world would turn to him, El Dashiki, not to the present leaders who had brought nothing but defeat, misery, and hunger to their people for the past twenty years. His one ambition would soon be realised and he would be supreme ruler of all Arabs.

The long period of training in Russia had paid dividends, enabling El Dashiki to set up an Intelligence network overseas. For almost two years his London agents sent little useful knowledge, then one day came the jackpot — the means to achieve his objective: KX4, the latest and most deadly germ-warfare weapon, was to be transported to Australia via Beirut.

It had been like taking candy from a baby and he prided himself on the smoothness of the operation. Only one man had discovered the identity of the hijacker — British agent Carlyle, and he hadn't lived long enough to talk.

The British had underestimated El Dashiki. He had learned much about their Intelligence while in Russia and Carlyle had been a warning: he had to trim down the opposition as much as possible and his London agents were ordered to act. But he had heard nothing from them since then. Maybe they had gone into hiding; maybe they had been picked up. He didn't really care. If they had been caught it was a small price to pay for such a valuable prize.

All he needed now was a good arsenal of arms to augment his attack on Israel. Russia had refused to sell to him and China had also turned a deaf ear. Now he was left with the pitifully few remains of arms that had either been stolen or bought off second-rate, small-time gun-runners. Money was no object; it had been flooding in from wealthy sympathisers all over the Arab world and, together with the fortune he had accumulated as a big-time crime operator, his assets amounted to millions. Someone had to rise to the bait eventually, and that someone was now on his way.

'If she is an agent then the British are even more stupid than I thought.'

He was a big, slovenly man with the crinkly, untidy beard now such an essential part of revolutionaries and freedom fighters. He sat back, feet on desk, tracing a strong hand over the short woollen tunic he always wore — the African dashiki that had given birth to his new name. He looked across at the man opposite: Hussein Jadid, former Captain of the Syrian Army, now his second in command.

'I see no other reason for a woman to accompany Smith on a business deal,' the Syrian explained. 'He is known to be fond of women but has never done such a thing before.'

El Dashiki laughed and wiped his heavy, negroid face with his shirt cuff.

'Maybe you are right and she thinks she will walk out of here with the germs in her handbag.'

Jadid sighed anxiously and glanced down at the photograph on the desk. He was short and stocky; clean shaven, with round, black eyes. His uniform was neat and well-fitting, a contrast to the other man's frayed creases and stains. He looked out of place in a guerrilla's hillside hideout.

'What will you do with her — if she is the British agent?'

'Go along with her at first, of course: play her game. Our need for arms is such that we cannot afford to do otherwise. Smith has a first-class reputation; maybe the deal is on the level and she is just using him to get to us. The moment she enters this room we will know who she is. If she is Mrs Marieanne Payne I doubt very much that Smith knows he is helping British Intelligence.'

He picked the photograph up.

'I think we will be able to arrange an unfortunate accident for her, should the need arise.' A grin broke across his face.

'Of course, we won't rush things — our men need a little amusement.'

He leaned back on his chair, slipped the photograph under his tunic into his shirt pocket, then looked around the crude office at the pictures pasted and taped to the whitewashed rock wall behind him and the partitioning: Castro, Che Guevara, Fanon, and Mao Tse-Tung. Details of doctrine didn't matter — the mere fact of being a revolutionary was credit enough to climb high in El Dashiki's esteem.

★   ★   ★

The sun had risen swiftly over the peaks from Israel and pushed a chilly daybreak towards the distant Lebanese coast. Its rich warmth bathed the landscape, burnishing bushes and trees with coppery and golden brilliance. Mount Hermon slowly emerged from the blackness of night into the shades and contrasts of day.

The two Jeeps pulled off the rough track and crossed the large, flat area below the hills. At first glance everywhere seemed deserted, but Marieanne hadn't missed the glint of metal and slight movement in the bushes. High in the side of the hills two sentries revealed themselves for a moment.

There was no sign of any caves. Camouflage and the nature of the terrain made them undetectable; it wasn't until they had laboured up another, narrower track to a small plateau that the openings were visible.

Smith crossed over and helped Marieanne to the ground. The young Syrian led them to the nearest cave.

'My God, but it's certainly big enough,' Smith commented.

The cave was divided into a battery of rooms by crude partitioning. A long corridor ran down the middle illuminated by a line of lights that dangled from the whitewashed rock ceiling. It certainly wasn't Sandhurst, but a distinct military atmosphere prevailed and, from behind one of the many olive-green doors, a typewriter clicked hesitantly under unskilled fingers.

They were ushered into a room close to the entrance.

'You wait here,' the young soldier said in slow, halting English. He hesitated before leaving and turned back to them.

'Have you any guns? Our leader is nervous of armed strangers. They will be returned before you leave.'

They handed their revolvers over and Marieanne hated the naked feeling of the empty holster. All she had left was the small stiletto sheathed inside the leg of her jeans.

The soldier left and a key turned in the lock.

Smith tried the door.

'We're locked in. Cautious bastards, aren't they?'

Marieanne nodded. The only furniture in the room was a frail table and two chairs.

Smith paced around for a moment then stood in front of a large photograph on the wall.

'I suppose this is our Beloved Leader.'

'That, my ill-informed friend, is Frantz Fanon or, should I say, was.'

'And who the hell was he?'

'He was a negro psychiatrist born in

Martinique — a big supporter of the Algerian revolution. He wrote *The Wretched of the Earth*. Most of these freedom fighters look up to him and his book as their primary example and inspiration.'

Smith moved close; his arms circled her waist.

'Quite a little know-all aren't you? Your pretty little head's full of facts, figures, and statistics. It's not natural and I don't like it.'

Marieanne smiled up at him.

'What kind of women *do* you like?' she asked.

'I didn't say I didn't like *you*, I just don't like what's in there.' He tapped her head.

The door opened and the young guerrilla re-entered. He gave Marieanne another wink and dazzling exposure of white teeth.

'El Dashiki will see you both now.'

He led them deeper into the cave and stopped at a door guarded by two soldiers. One guard knocked, entered, and announced the visitors.

Marieanne and Smith walked in and the door closed behind them. The man nearest stood, clicked his heels, then sat down again, smoothing well-pressed trousers over his knees. The other remained slouched in his chair, feet still on the desk, picking his teeth with a broken matchstick. The mass of black, frizzy hair stood almost upright around his head and his dark skin shone. He stared briefly from Marieanne to Smith then fixed his gaze back on the girl as he scratched his armpit under the worn, brown dashiki.

'Mr Hitchin Smith,' he eventually began, 'And Ma'mseille Lessard, I believe.'

He turned back to the Englishman.

'I am pleased to welcome you at last and must apologise for my men not being able to meet you earlier: as you may know, we had trouble in the night and I gather you also had unwelcome visitors. But, before we talk business, I must introduce you to my second-in-command, Captain Jadid.'

Again the other man stood and clicked his heels.

There was a knock at the door. A young boy entered, carrying four mugs on a tin lid. He handed the coffee round then left. Marieanne sat by Jadid; Smith stood by the desk. They waited for El Dashiki to speak but he gazed at them in silence whilst chewing the matchstick he had picked his teeth with and blowing and sipping his drink noisily.

Yasir Abu-Hashi's previous mental pictures of female intelligence agents were rather confused: they were either overpoweringly sophisticated, expensively dressed, and heavily made up, or completely masculine horrors, in shapeless tweeds, with dark fuzz on the top lip. Now these earlier ideas were shattered and he surveyed Marieanne leisurely from top to toe. Her dark hair was tied back, but the fringe revealed in the photograph was missing — no doubt pushed up under the black hairband. Her young face was completely free of cosmetics. He admired the slender body clothed in close-fitting denim; saw the slight rise of a small breast under the tee-shirt and pressed his tongue against the matchstick that had wedged between two teeth. He pushed it free then spat it out. Her photograph hadn't done her justice: she was beautiful — very beautiful — but she had to die — after providing a pleasurable night for himself and his men. He had been in exclusively male company for too long. Faced with this girl he realised his need and the prospects of touching her white skin excited him. She would fight him — it would be no good if she didn't. He would laugh at her revulsion towards his black skin. Then he would take her. He would hurt her and laugh at her pain. There would be no fight left in her when he gave her to the others.

Marieanne stared back at him, enthralled and revolted by his slovenly appearance and bad manners.

'These arms you have for me, Mr Smith: what do they consist of?'

Smith pulled a brown envelope from inside his jacket and handed the contents over.

'It is a complete list with breakdown of prices,' he said.

Captain Jadid moved behind the desk and looked over his leader's shoulder. They studied the list together and Marieanne noticed the hint of a smile that formed on El Dashiki's thick lips. Then he stood up and began to pace the room, still reading. He was tall, at least six-foot two or three, and broad.

'It is indeed an impressive selection, Smith: Howitzers from Finland, anti-aircraft guns from America, Belgian carbines and machine guns, bazookas from Britain, American and French sub-machine guns, and American and Italian side arms.'

He rolled the list into a tube, looked down it, blew into it, then tapped his beard with it.

'Tell me, how did you acquire such a collection?'

Smith lit a cigarette. For the first time he had no idea how the weapons he was selling had been acquired. He decided to toss the ball into the other court.

'I am just employed as agent in this transaction. The arms belong to Miss Lessard's employer. If she wishes to tell you then that's her business.'

El Dashiki turned to Marieanne and sensed the calculating mind behind the cool gaze as she spoke to him.

'If the arms are acceptable to you and the price is right, what difference does it make where they come from? After all, my employer doesn't wish to know where you got the money from to pay for them.'

For a moment anger shadowed his face, then he burst into loud laughter.

'You are right of course, Ma'mseille. So long as I get good weapons it is no concern of mine where you have got them from. The price is high but I am satisfied, subject to a demonstration. I trust Mr Smith's judgment and he must be satisfied with you and your boss. Tell me, where are the arms now and how soon will I be able to take delivery?'

'They are on a ship due in Sour tonight,' Smith replied. 'The arms will be loaded on to trucks and could be here by morning.'

El Dashiki rubbed his chin.

'But that might not be so simple, my friend. The authorities here have officially banned guerrilla forces. Arms would not be allowed to be unloaded.'

'All that has been taken care of,' Marieanne assured him. 'There will be no difficulties at all.'

That was Johnny's department: a little bribery and blackmail always worked wonders.

'Then I must compliment you and your organisation on your efficiency. Now I want to see the samples demonstrated. Then we will settle the deal.'

Marieanne stood.

'If you will excuse me I should like to rest for a while. Mr Smith will take care of everything for you.'

Smith looked up and marvelled at her self-confidence. El Dashiki's belief in his satisfaction was far from being correct; Smith was *not* satisfied: all he had as tangible evidence of the deal were the samples and events so far. Further than that he was blindly taking Marieanne's word. Was there a ship with arms on board? Overpowering panics of doubt and frightening possibilities had been settling into his mind since the journey from Beirut airport. He had tried to push them aside but now they loomed up before him again: Marieanne was part of a confidence trick. She was going to take El

Dashiki for all he had and somewhere there would be someone else — her boss, her husband, her lover, or her brother. What a fool he was not to have ditched her at the Hilton.

★   ★   ★

Marieanne was shown to their room by the sex-starved Syrian who made it clear that he wanted to stay and what he wanted to stay for. She made it clear that she wasn't interested and eventually the threat of reporting him to his leader put an end to his persistence. He left, slamming and locking the door ferociously.

The room was as austere as the others and housed two bunks and one small table. She lay down and reflected on the past few days. Now she had to find where El Dashiki was keeping KX4 and it didn't seem likely that it would be in the camp.

She wondered how Johnny's arrangements had worked out at the other end. He was in Sour, luxuriating in a secluded British Embassy-owned villa, waiting for her to contact him. Lucky bastard! She envied him and allowed herself the luxury of an imaginary hot shower, good food, and soft, cool sheets.

At first there was a lot of noise and activity from inside the cave but gradually it quietened and she waited, sleep almost overtaking her, until all had been completely silent for fifteen minutes.

Then the distant burst of machine-gun fire snatched her back to full consciousness. The demonstration was in progress. She got off the bunk, took a long hairpin from her bag, and crossed over to the door. She unlocked it in less than a minute and peered cautiously out into the corridor. Everywhere appeared to be deserted so she walked down to El Dashiki's office. The door was unlocked and she went inside.

She searched through the drawers, the filing cabinet, and the cupboard. Much of the paperwork was written both in French and Arabic and consisted almost entirely of propaganda. There were no clues as to the whereabouts of KX4.

On the floor behind the desk was his

safe. She knelt in front of it and ran her fingers over the dial for a few seconds, realising the futility of attempting to find the correct combination by trial and error. Then she looked up and Mao Tse-tung smiled affably down at her from the wall directly above the safe. She smiled back at him.

'I'll bet you're the key, you sly old Chinese goat.'

The fingers of her right hand cautiously moved the dial. The safe opened.

It was crammed with money from top to bottom. She took some out, sorted amongst the bundles and made a rough estimate as to the total amount: at least two million pounds, with approximately two thirds in American dollars and the rest in sterling.

'If Harold Wilson could see all this . . . ' Then Marieanne's mind turned to selfish thoughts: here was a till well worth dipping into. The Master need never know El Dashiki carried so much cash; she only had to account for one million, plus a little, just to show she was honest. The rest could be divided between herself, Hitchin, and Johnny.

She made a final check that the safe contained nothing other than money, put the thick wads back, then locked the door. After a quick look round for another possible hiding place she left the office and walked to the entrance of the cave. Looking down into the valley from the small plateau, she saw that the demonstration was still in progress. The whole guerrilla group clustered together as a machine gun ripped into the remains of a deserted homestead. She watched for a moment then walked back and made a swift tour of each room and the other, smaller caves. As expected, there was no sign or evidence of KX4.

* * *

She awoke slowly, conscious of rough blankets against her naked body. She was warm and threw them back, stretching her hand towards the table for her watch, but was unable to reach it. She got up and crossed the room, which was in pitch darkness. Her fingers traced over the wall until she found the light switch and turned it on.

'Oh, now that's nice!'

She turned. Smith was sitting up on the other bunk, his gold medallion swaying before his chest.

'Is he going to buy?' she asked and rubbed her eyes.

Smith leaned back on his elbows and smiled in sheer admiration. Her body was perfect. The small breasts were firm and erectile, balanced by slender hips and thighs. She saw the pleasure in his face and walked over to him, proudly and tauntingly displaying herself.

'Look, darling, if you want to talk business cover yourself up a little. Otherwise all you'll get from me is sex.'

She pulled a blanket over her shoulders, wrapped it round herself, then knelt on the end of his bunk.

'Is that better?'

He smiled, leaned forward and pushed her hair back from her face.

'Yes. For some reason I cannot mix naked female flesh with business discussions. I get distracted somewhere along the line.'

'Tell me about El Dashiki.'

'He *is* going to buy.'

'Good. And payment?'

'Cash on delivery.'

She wished she could tell him about the two million in the safe; the expression on his face would have been quite something. Instead she looked at her watch on the table: it was almost six o'clock.

'I shall have to leave for Sour soon.'

'El Dashiki is providing an escort for you. He doesn't want us both to go.'

She had intended going alone and told him so.

'Well, you bloody well can't. Our beloved leader is most insistent. Besides, it's dangerous to go travelling alone in these parts — especially at night.'

She looked so vulnerable; the long, loose hair tumbled over the dark-grey blanket. A slender arm smoothed the drab wool over her knees.

Why did she want to go alone? Again doubts nagged Smith. For a while he said nothing and Marieanne sensed the anxiety as his dark, sleepy eyes evaded hers. She didn't like what she was doing to him. Hitchin Smith had spent many years building himself into what he was — probably the most trusted one-man-operation gunrunner in the world. Like royalty, he was above politics and, by reason of his reputation, many countries had placed him above the law. Now she was dragging him into something that could ruin him.

She asked his thoughts.

He looked into her face.

'If you really want to know the truth, Marieanne, I'm not sure whether I trust you or not.'

'Why?'

'You act like a professional killer, not a wholesaler's assistant.'

'I have killed to make sure this deal goes through.'

'Deal? I'm beginning to doubt there is a deal.'

Again coldness flowed into her eyes.

'And what exactly *do* you think, Hitchin?'

He told her.

'I'm not conning him,' she flung back.

'The arms will be in Sour tonight.'

'I bloody well hope so — or else we'll both be dead ducks.'

Marieanne moved up the bunk; her hand touched his shoulder.

'You must trust me, Hitchin.'

The touch of her fingertips and the soft voice pierced his emotions. Slowly he turned his eyes up to hers. They gazed back into his invitingly, like two dark pools of erotic promise. The nights of deprivation aboard the airliner and out in the chilly countryside under Ali Baba's gaze intensified his immediate need. Clutching her shoulders he pulled her down to him, kissing her roughly and forgetting his doubts.

Then she wriggled out of the blanket like a warm kitten and lay beside him. Her eyes closed and she smiled as his hands moved over her body.

'Is this going to strengthen your waning trust in me?'

'I don't know,' he muttered, 'but it certainly isn't going to strengthen me.'

His face pressed against her breasts and he felt the tremor of emotion as his lips caressed them. Then she pushed him back against the pillow and moved over him. Her hair fell on to his face and the contours of her body moved rhythmically against his. She laughed softly and bit the lobe of his ear.

A sudden surge of jealousy overtook Smith; he grabbed her hair and pulled it painfully.

'Is there someone else? There must be. You're going to see him tonight, aren't you?'

A girl like her had to belong to someone.

'Tell me!'

'I don't like such self-righteous demands,' she answered testily. 'They belong to a tired marriage. Besides, a few nights ago a certain Italian lady lay panting in your arms.'

The momentary anger faded and she laughed, her fingertips tracing his features. Then they worked through his thick hair and she slid her tongue lightly over his lips.

'I'm sorry, Marieanne, but you make me want exclusive rights.'

And Hitchin Smith had never bothered about exclusive rights before. He moved from beneath her and turned her on to her back.

'It's my turn first. Clever as you undoubtedly are, my love, there are some things best left to me.'

Her eyes were wide and bright then closed contentedly as they became one. Smith felt himself locked in her arms and legs and he didn't care about the other strange feeling that had worried him for the last few days — a feeling he'd never experienced before: he wasn't going to tire of her — ever.

* * *

Captain Jadid and a Palestinian guerrilla were delegated to accompany Marieanne to Sour. Smith stood beside El Dashiki and watched the Jeep drive out into the night. He wondered why such a superior officer as Jadid had been chosen and asked the guerrilla leader. El Dashiki turned, asked him to repeat the question, then laughed. He laughed until tears ran down his cheeks.

'What's the big joke?' Smith asked.

El Dashiki paused and pointed a finger at him.

'What's the joke, you ask,' his voice boomed. 'Mr Smith, I think you are one very big fool.'

The Englishman's features set like stone.

'You really don't know, do you?' Again he roared with laughter.

'I don't know *what?*' Smith shouted.

An inquisitive crowd of freedom fighters gathered around them, echoing their leader's laughter without knowing the reason for it.

El Dashiki wiped the tears from his eyes with the ragged dashiki.

'Your beautiful girl friend is a British secret agent.'

There was a short, electric silence.

'Rubbish! Why would a British agent help me sell arms to you of all people?'

'Because, my foolish friend, I have something that belongs to the British and they have, no doubt, sent her to find it. You have been used as her ticket to me.'

'I don't believe it!'

However, Smith did believe it, but knew he had to protect her.

'I'm afraid there is no doubt about it, Mr Smith. Now we shall soon see whether this arms business is on the level. And you had better start praying, for your own sake, that I do get them. Maybe the British Government thinks it worth such a deal in order to try to get their precious possession back.'

Smith asked what it was but he wouldn't say.

'And what will you do with Miss Lessard?'

'You mean Mrs Payne — Marieanne Payne? I will do nothing yet. If there are arms I want them. Then I will deal with her.'

He began to walk away and Smith kicked a stone and stared down at the ground. No wonder she had changed her name. No wonder she was a crack shot and judo expert. No wonder she hadn't a nerve in her body. No wonder she gave herself to him so freely. Cheating, lying little bitch! He kicked another stone viciously.

El Dashiki turned.

'I don't know what your relationship is with Mrs Payne but you won't be given the opportunity to help her in any way.'

'I shall want to see her — as soon as she gets back,' Smith stated.

'Maybe.' The Arab smiled slowly. 'She is the first woman many of my men have seen for a long time. They would think me extremely inconsiderate if I killed her straight away. Yes, my stupid friend, you can see her — you can watch.'

He gave a signal and Smith turned. Two soldiers walked towards him. He was pushed at gun point towards the cave.

6

The bar was full; at least a dozen Mediterranean and Arab nationalities made up the bawdy crowd. They stared at the belly dancer in greedy appreciation. She was provoking a fat, French sailor with the sensuous twisting of her body and bell-tipped fingers, allowing her hips to brush against his arm as she moved close.

Aromatic smoke coiled towards the grey ceiling, shrouding the light which hung from elaborate ironwork fittings. At the back of the bar men stood in the shadows of tall, curved alcoves, their bodies silhouetted against the colourful mosaic walls. An accompaniment of tapping feet supported the heady Arab rhythm and its swirling, swaying, intense beat filled the room.

The dancer twisted away from the sweaty Frenchman; his friends cheered and laughed, and tried to push him off his seat. Her body moved with serpentine ease across the floor, jewelled feet swishing over shiny tiles. Her dark eyes searched through the crowd until they rested on the young European. She moved towards him, as she had the previous night, and dedicated her dance to him, hoping he would again smile promisingly.

The European leaned back against the bar and watched her. He was slim, not tall, with beautiful features that fascinated the Arab girl. Slender fingers tapped his glass and the light caught the thick gold chain round his wrist. He wore sand-coloured trousers and battle jacket, contrasted by a fine, brown sweater. His light-brown hair curled against the turtle neck and waved over his forehead and ears.

Her body twisted and turned for him alone, swinging the long chiffon skirt out from generous hips. Her curtain of glossy black hair tossed back and forward with the movement of her head. It was hot and beads of perspiration slipped down between her full breasts under the green jewelled top. She smiled at him, opened her eyes wide, then closed them, running her tongue over full, red lips.

Johnny Armstrong admired her delicious curves and the flexing and relaxing of supple muscles. Her skin was smooth and dusky. He smiled, still very much aware of the night before. Again he saw the open invitation; but tonight she would be disappointed. Knowing Marieanne would soon be with him, he felt no desire to re-indulge himself in the dancer's warm and eager body.

Movement in the doorway diverted his attention: Marieanne stepped through the bead curtain. She looked around, saw Johnny and crossed over to him. He signalled the barman and ordered a drink.

His face gave no indication of emotion, but he had missed her: he always missed her.

'Hard at work — as usual,' Marieanne greeted. 'I can see why you chose *this* bar.'

She nodded towards the dancer.

Johnny took the brandy and handed it to her. She still wore the denim two-piece but had a black sweater under it. Her hair was tied in bunches with two small tortoiseshell clips and her cheeks were pink from the windy drive.

'I can assure you, darling, on top of all the work I've done at this end, you haven't been far out of my sights since yesterday morning.'

'And last night? I take it this is either a dance of gratitude or indication of availability.'

'Both actually,' he answered. 'I felt I deserved a night off and left your nocturnal welfare up to Smith.'

'I would hardly have called it a night *off*, Johnny.' She smiled at the dancer whose eyes flashed jealous fire. Then the dance was over and she swept past them and flounced through another bead curtain. Her exit marked Jadid's entrance and he strode over to them with the Palestinian soldier close on his heels. They looked unimpressive in civilian clothes; the Syrian Captain could have passed for a bank manager or prosperous merchant in his cream linen suit and silk shirt.

Marieanne introduced them and, in an American accent, Johnny announced himself as an associate of Miss Lessard, Mike Gibson. He felt cheated, having intended taking Marieanne to his villa for an hour before the arms were unloaded.

Jadid was ill at ease and glanced suspiciously around the bar.

'Is everything all right?' he asked.

Johnny nodded:

'Sure. As soon as we get to the wharf your arms will be unloaded.'

'Then may we go there at once, Mr Gibson? My presence in public could lead to trouble: the army have agents everywhere.'

★   ★   ★

The port of Sour, better known by its ancient name of Tyre, has changed little in four thousand years. Once an important Phoenician port, it stands on a rocky island close to the mainland. Alexander the Great was only able to take the town, after seven months of siege, by building a great dyke, linking it to the shore. Now time and the sea has turned the dyke into an isthmus.

Marieanne sat with Johnny in the E-type Jaguar he had hired. The Jeep was parked about four yards away. Jadid and his subordinate stared irritably across at them, unable to hear their conversation.

With infuriating slowness the ship's derricks moved into action. There were no officials to interfere — a blanket of bribe money had temporarily closed down all formalities.

Marieanne ran through events so far, but Johnny was already aware of most of them.

'El Dashiki has a couple of 122mm. Russian guns hidden at the top of the hills,' he told her. 'I had a look yesterday. Everybody was too busy watching Smith's demonstration to notice. I also met Smith's mate, Ali Baba, on the way out. He was waiting by the plane for spare parts to arrive from Beirut, cursing those bandits for tampering with the engine.'

Marianne laughed.

'Poor devil!'

'I think I'll follow you back,

145

Marieanne. We have to get El Dashiki away from his hideout and make him tell us where KX4 is.'

He handed her a cigarette, lit it, then slid his arm round her shoulder. Jadid and the Palestinian continued to gaze across and Johnny stared back.

'They're either suspicious or just two sneaky little voyeurs,' he muttered. 'To satisfy them maybe I should make love to you in some devastatingly devious position. After all, they *have* sort of ballsed up my plans for you tonight.'

But instead they formed a plan of action and discussed it as the packing cases were lowered on to the wharf.

'How's Smith shaping?'

'Very well,' Marieanne answered. 'He's quite capable of looking after himself and can fight like the devil.'

'We've had him under observation for some time. We want him to work for us — on a part-time basis, of course.'

She turned to him.

'My God, I should have known, shouldn't I? You certainly want your pound of flesh from him.'

'We don't want a pound of flesh, love — we want all of him. He will be a valuable asset to the Department.'

'He'll never agree to do Service work, Johnny. When he finds out who I am, and what this is all about, he'll just about hit the roof.'

'Oh, I think he will work for us, Marieanne. If he refuses he'll never sell another gun anywhere in the world: his name will be mud — to say the least.'

She said nothing and turned away. There was a short silence until Johnny twisted her round to him, his fingers digging painfully into her arms.

'And how is our swinging gunrunner treating you?' His voice was cynical, his eyes piercingly bright.

'Perfectly.' She smiled.

'I'm so glad of that. Tell me, is he a better or a worse lover than I am?'

He pulled her to him, his lips crushed against hers then moved over the warm cheek to her ear. He bit the soft lobe gently and whispered her name once. Marieanne breathed in his perfume and could feel his hair against her face. Then she turned her head; her fingers covered bitter eyes that stared into hers, exposing the jealousy he would never admit to. He took her hands and held them tight. For a moment he looked at her then closed his eyes, remembering events years before — that could have been aeons in the past.

He had first met Marieanne at a party. She was eighteen and had just left school. They were instantly attracted to each other, the one as beautiful, intelligent, and self-assured as the other. Johnny's high academic standards were, like hers, untapped assets and his only ambition was to paint. An affair started that shocked his parents and deprived Marieanne of her virginity within twenty-four hours. Her father's only reaction had been to shrug and express relief that fourteen years of convents hadn't deprived her of all human feelings and weaknesses.

A week later Johnny took her back to Paris where he had lived since finishing an unwilling two-year commission in the Navy. For three months they lived together in a sunny studio, made love and talked of marriage and children. Johnny painted and earned a living of sorts for them both. But, secretly, he battled with himself: his father constantly badgered him to stop bumming around and to take a secure government job, like any self-respecting son of an admiral would do. For a long time he had plugged his wayward son's many academic talents throughout the Ministries, his efforts eventually resulting in Johnny being approached in Paris. For a week he ran the offer through his mind. Then he took Marieanne into his confidence and a decision was reached. The next day they flew back to London and began the two years' training course with the Department.

That had been nine years before. Now Marieanne was twenty-seven and Johnny thirty-three. Apart from the two years of her marriage they had been constant lovers, but now there was no talk of marriage and children.

He opened his eyes and held her to him again: they were both conscious of emotions that couldn't be satisfied on a Lebanese dockyard under the close gaze of two Arabs.

'Well?' he reminded her of his demand.

She smiled. To Johnny love was an elaborate and skilful art, to be studied thoroughly and practised with great expertise and precision. To Smith it was an impulsive and happy romp.

'He's different,' she whispered. 'But he's all right and deserves a cut of the other million.'

'If and when we get it,' he added and released her. He sat back and banged his fist lightly against the steering wheel.

'There's always the chance El Dashiki knows who you are, love. The Israelis obviously do.'

He took a revolver from the glove compartment and slipped it into her empty holster. In silence they watched the unloading and Marieanne leaned against his shoulder, twisting the gold chain slowly round his wrist. The two guerrillas still watched them studiously.

Ten minutes later the fleet of hired trucks rumbled on to the wharf.

'What did you say you wanted them for?' Marieanne asked.

'I didn't say anything, darling, and the

guy didn't ask; he was too overcome with joy when I slipped him a fat backhander.' He grinned then added softly, 'He'll be even more overcome tomorrow: I doubt very much whether he'll ever see his precious bloody trucks again.'

* * *

Jadid insisted on random cases being opened and checked before allowing Johnny to supervise the loading and it was nearly twelve-thirty before the consignment was finally packed into the covered trucks. The Lebanese drivers huddled in a circle playing dice by the wharf edge. The ship's crew went below decks and the handful of dock workers left.

'What time will the balloon go up?' Marieanne whispered to Johnny.

He looked at his watch.

'Three — if there are no hold-ups.'

They turned back and walked back to Jadid for the O.K. to go.

But two revolvers levelled at them.

'Put your hands up and turn round.'

151

Jadid's voice was low. The drivers couldn't see the guns as their view was blocked by Johnny and Marieanne. They carried on their game ignorant of the situation.

'You thought you could fool us, Mrs Payne. I expect this gentleman is a British agent also. Now, fortunately for us, we shall have both KX4 *and* the arms — and our leader will have no need to pay for these weapons. He will be able to keep his one million pounds for other things.'

The Palestinian took Johnny's gun, pushed it into his pocket, then stood in front of Marieanne. He took her gun, but his hands lingered and greedily moved over her sweater and jeans. He grinned and muttered lewdly in Arabic. Marieanne closed her eyes and held her breath; his face was oily and he smelt of stale sweat. Johnny's face froze with rage but he didn't move: neither of them could afford to protest.

A sharp order from Jadid brought the guerrilla to heel. He stepped back, still grinning.

Another lorry rumbled on to the wharf

and about two dozen of El Dashiki's men jumped down. At rifle point the Lebanese drivers were bound, gagged, and blindfolded, then pushed into the empty lorry.

'What about us?' Johnny felt he should ask at that point.

'El Dashiki will be more than pleased to entertain you both. When the arms have been safely delivered we will take the drivers far from our camp and release them.'

Jadid's chest puffed with pride at his successful coup and his beady, black eyes flashed triumph.

'Of course, you two will not be so fortunate.' He stepped up to Marieanne and pushed his face close to hers. 'You, especially, will be sorry,' he hissed.

Marieanne found his B class movie melodrama quite ridiculous and smiled.

'You will not find it so amusing when we get back to our leader,' he snapped.

She bit her bottom lip.

El Dashiki's men commandeered the trucks. One guerrilla climbed into the driver's seat of the Jeep. Johnny and Marieanne were pushed into the back;

Jadid and the Palestinian sat opposite them, revolvers still poised.

Jadid laughed.

'You should see yourselves. The two big, clever, British agents. Not so clever now, are you?'

He repeated his remarks in Arabic. The other man sniggered and they muttered together.

'Mrs Payne, my soldier asks if he can have you when we get back. I have told him you will be available. Of course, though, he will take his turn with the others.'

She ignored the threat. They both sat complacently — a convincing picture of moody surrender. Angry reaction would probably result in them being tied up, making escape impossible.

The trucks began to move. The Jeep followed the last one off the wharf, through the deserted back streets of Sour, then over the isthmus and into the countryside.

Marieanne looked out for Smith's plane as she had earlier, but the airstrip was too far off the road to be seen at night.

The driver was hopeless; his lack of skill and confidence soon caused them to fall far behind the convoy. Jadid shouted and cursed him, threatening dire punishments. Between Tibnine and Bent Jebail the road worsened and so did the driving. The Jeep pitched and tossed over deep ruts and gaping holes. By then, the trucks had been out of sight for some time.

Johnny looked at his watch: It was almost two a.m. He turned to Marieanne. Her face was expressionless, her eyes switched from Jadid to the Palestinian, then back to him.

'I'm hungry,' she muttered.

Their freedom was triggered by a deep rut just outside Bent Jebail. The Jeep's near side dropped down; Jadid fell forward. Johnny raised his right leg and kicked out. His shoe met the Syrian's jaw with such force there was a sharp crack of breaking bone.

The driver dragged at the wheel as he tried to steer the Jeep out of the rut.

Jadid sprawled unconscious across the floor, blood running from his distorted mouth. Johnny took his gun, pushed the

Palestinian back on to the opposite seat, then pressed it into the driver's neck, ordering him to stop.

The Palestinian stood, holding the side of the Jeep for support. He aimed his gun at Johnny but they were still careering through the rut and his hand wavered. Then the Jeep stopped, but he never fired: he screamed; the revolver clattered to the floor. Marieanne's knife had ripped into the inside of his wrist and blood spurted out. For a few seconds he stared at the blade embedded in his flesh, then dragged it free.

The driver turned, staring at them in horror, but Johnny's gun still dug into his neck.

The Palestinian flung himself at Marieanne, thrusting the knife towards her chest. She ducked, it slashed into the seat and his left hand grabbed her throat. Twisting away, she forced the knife back, easing his wrist round. His blood flowed warmly over her hand. Her other hand clawed at the fingers pressing painfully into her throat. One more twist and she forced his hand right round then pushed hard; the knife slid in between his ribs. At the same time there was a shot; he screamed; both hands clutched his head. He slid from her and slumped on top of Jadid, a thin trickle of blood running from behind his ear where Johnny had shot him.

Marieanne cleaned her knife on the corpse.

'Look,' she pointed. The driver had jumped to the ground and was sprinting back along the road, stumbling and tripping in his eagerness to get away.

'One dead, one wounded, and one deserter,' Johnny remarked. 'I think we'll increase those figures before daybreak.'

They took their guns from the Palestinian's pockets then hid the bodies behind a bush. Jadid was still unconscious.

After a struggle the Jeep was freed. They drove it back on to the road then sat together — hot, breathless and dusty. Johnny lit two cigarettes and handed one to Marieanne.

'Fortunately our plan isn't quite as buggered up as it might have been,' he sighed. His jacket was spattered with the Arab's blood. Marieanne's face was splashed and her right hand covered with it. He licked his handkerchief and wiped off as much as he could.

'At least you've been saved from a fate worse than death, love. Does that please or disappoint you?'

'I don't think I'd like to be raped by a whole army of Arab freedom fighters. None of them uses a deodorant.'

'The trouble with you, Marieanne, is that I've spoiled you: you're too bloody particular.'

They laughed; he ruffled her hair then started the engine.

'No doubt Smith's under lock and key by now,' he told her. 'Feeling very sorely disposed towards you. Get him out then carry on as we arranged. Don't stand any nonsense from him. I'll wait to pick you up — if the Israelis let me get back down.'

They didn't catch sight of the convoy again until almost at the foot of the hills.

'What about the Lebanese drivers?' Marieanne asked.

'They'll have to look after themselves. You can't afford to do more than you have to. Remember that, Marieanne.

You're only going to get Smith out because you need him — and the Department needs him.'

'I wouldn't leave him anyway,' she retorted.

'Oh, for Christ's sake, Marieanne, don't let's talk about fair play and all that junk; I might throw up.'

'At times I think you'd leave me, if it weren't for the fact that the Department needs me . . . '

'And the fact that I need you,' he put in.

She sat back and sighed.

'Maybe Smith won't have anything to do with me when I get back. After all, I've landed him in one hell of a mess, but he may have managed to come to some sort of an agreement with El Dashiki.'

'Well, if he won't play ball, you'll have to leave him, darling. And if he's really turned nasty — get rid of him. He's not so bloody indispensable yet that we should risk our necks to keep him in the party.'

Then they were close to the camp and drove across the plain. The last of the lorries laboured up the track and the others were packed together in front of the caves.

Johnny braked at the edge of the flat ground near the track.

'Out you get, girl.'

They checked their watches: it was two thirty-three.

'What time's zero hour now?' she asked.

'Three-thirty.'

She jumped down; he leaned over and held her hands tightly.

'Good luck, Marieanne; look after yourself, for God's sake.'

She nodded, wished him luck and he kissed her lips lightly.

For a moment he watched her walk towards the cave, darting from moonlight to shadow. Then he drove the Jeep up the path leading to El Dashiki's Russian heavy guns.

7

There wasn't enough room for the whole convoy in front of the caves and three trucks had been left at the top of the track. The last one held the Lebanese drivers.

Marieanne glanced at her watch and decided, as she had many times in the past, to disregard Johnny's instructions. She climbed into the back and untied the nearest driver. He blinked as she removed his blindfold and gag.

'Are you all right?' she whispered in French.

'Yes. What has happened?'

'We were hijacked. Unfasten the others; tell them not to make a sound, then one of you must get into the cab without being seen. At three-thirty you will hear heavy gunfire. When you do — you must reverse down the hill immediately and get away as fast as you can.'

'Where are we, Ma'mseille?'

'In the hills past Bent Jebail. You *must* get away quickly or all be killed.'

She stepped back and raised her hand. 'Good luck.'

'But what about you?' The man stood to help her. 'How will you get away?'

'Someone will pick me up. Don't worry.'

She took his hand and lowered herself to the ground.

'May God be with you,' the Lebanese wished fervently.

'I hope so as well,' she smiled and, using the three trucks as cover, walked towards the rowdy activity.

She peered round the front of the last truck. Like kids opening stockings and pillowcases on Christmas morning, the guerrillas were unloading their new arms; hysterical excitement ruined all attempts at efficiency; disorganisation reigned supreme. Boxes were being passed down and lifted from all the trucks available to them, lids were impatiently prised open and straw and packing materials blew around.

There was no sign of Smith.

El Dashiki stood in the middle of the

mêlée, powerful arms folded across his chest. For a moment he watched as his men showed him rifles, ammunition and grenades. Then his strong voice bellowed out and everyone began to clear a space for one of the field guns to be unloaded. Their backs were towards Marieanne.

She darted over to the large cave and crouched in a shadow at the side of the entrance. The long corridor leading deep into the hill was deserted. She stepped in and hurried down to the room she and Smith had occupied. It was unlocked. She shut the door behind her and turned on the light. Where was Smith? Their baggage was still there and she opened her old airline bag: nothing had been taken, but it had been hurriedly searched and the cosmetics, toilet articles, tee-shirt and other things were all jumbled together. She emptied the entire contents into Smith's holdall which she placed by the door before leaving.

No one appeared to be in the cave and, with the empty bag slung over her shoulder, she tried a few doors. All the rooms were unlocked.

It was five to three and the guerrillas were still noisily involved with their new toys to the right of the cave entrance. If one stepped back a few yards Marieanne would be in clear view.

She opened the door at the far end of the corridor and shut herself in the small room. A table, chair and cupboard furnished it and another door faced her — a heavy wooden door with a small grille. She crossed over quietly and peered in.

Hitchin Smith lay on the bunk of the cell, blowing smoke rings up to the ceiling.

'Is that all you have to do with your time?'

He sat up. His first reaction was relief but immediately it soured into anger.

'Yes — thanks to you, you stupid, cheating little bitch.' He walked slowly to the door. 'And that wealthy American boss who doesn't exist.'

'You need a shave, Hitchin.' She smiled broadly then searched through the cupboard and drawer. There was no key.

'I'll soon get you out,' she went on.

'Then you can start to earn your cut again — and possibly a great deal more on the side.'

She crouched by the door.

It wasn't an easy lock to pick and Smith continually expressed his lack of faith in her efforts.

'You'll never do it — mucking about with a bloody hairpin. Like a third-rate spy film.'

'Maybe I'm a third-rate spy.'

'You can say that again!'

She pushed the door open. Smith shrugged, put his suede jacket on and ground his cigarette into the floor.

'You cheated and lied to me, Marieanne.'

'Yes I know I did, but we'll talk about that later.'

'What's wrong with right now?'

'Because in less than half an hour this whole place is going to resemble Custer's Last Stand.'

He followed her into the corridor.

'What's all that racket outside?'

'The arms are being unloaded. You know — those arms you didn't believe existed.'

She picked up his holdall from behind the door and handed it to him.

Six Israeli Uzi assault rifles lay in the cupboard in El Dashiki's office, each fully loaded with twenty-five rounds. Marieanne took two, along with spare ammunition.

'And be ready to use it,' she warned, throwing one over to Smith.

'Would you mind telling me what all this is about?' he snapped.

'Well, for a start I'm going to open the safe and empty it.'

'How — with a hairpin again?' He smiled patronisingly.

'No, I'll use the combination.'

'Oh, so I gather El Dashiki leaves it pinned to the wall on a sheet of paper just in case he has a visit from a spy.'

'How did you guess? It's here.' She pointed to the photo of Mao Tse-tung. 'The combination is his birthday; date, month, and year. I opened it yesterday. There are two million pounds in it and I only have to account for half that amount.'

Again Smith shrugged. Marieanne had ceased to amaze him. She opened the safe and he knelt beside her. Together they filled her bag and crammed the rest into his.

Then Marieanne looked at her watch.

'Fifteen minutes left,' she muttered.

'Then what happens?'

She shut the safe and told him.

'Jesus! We'll never get out alive!'

'We will, but not until we've got El Dashiki.'

'What do we need him for?' He grabbed her arm. 'Listen to me, Marieanne, I want to know *right now* what we're here for.'

It took almost the full fifteen minutes to give him a condensed version of her mission, the reason for it, and what had happened since she left him the previous evening.

'Why did you lie?' he demanded. 'Why didn't you tell me about the bloody germs in the first place.'

'I couldn't tell you until you were too deeply involved to back out. You would never have agreed to the deal if you had had the slightest glimmering of the truth, would you?'

'No, I bloody well wouldn't!'

He looked at her. She stood by the desk, the bulging bag slung across her chest, and the gun held firmly. She was waiting and listening, frequently looking at her watch. There was a smear of blood near her ear and her skin was pale. She yawned and rubbed her nose. Then she looked up at him and her dark eyes were shadowed with tiredness. At that moment he both hated and admired her.

'Behind the door,' she said. 'There's less than two minutes left.'

He followed her and they stood close, watching the second hand of her watch.

'Did sleeping with me mean nothing to you?' he asked. 'Did some sick little civil servant order you to seduce me? Was it difficult to pretend pleasure and satisfaction?'

'I *was* ordered to seduce you, Hitchin, but the pleasure and satisfaction were for real, I can assure you.'

She smiled but Smith's eyes remained cold and scornful. His ego had been completely demolished.

It was three-thirty.

Johnny reached the ridge of the hill and stepped out of the Jeep, pulling his collar up against a cold wind that hurled masses of cloud across the moon. Total darkness came and went frequently. It was almost quarter to three.

The gun was concealed in a deep fissure, completely covered with camouflage. Everything was as the day before and half a dozen cases of shells and charges were stacked against the side of the fissure.

He stood in front of the gun and looked down into Israel. When the moon broke through the clouds he could just see his target — an Israeli border post. For a moment he looked down at it, wondering how many deaths he was going to cause, but he wasn't really sure whether he cared or not: in the last seven years he'd been the cause of countless deaths.

Then he climbed on to the gun, checked it and was agreeably surprised at its condition. It was well greased and clean. He manoeuvred it and rehearsed his aim after making a few mental calculations. When satisfied he jumped down, took his jacket off and walked over to the ammunition. Each 122mm. shell was a formidable weight: firing a gun that size was never intended to be a one-man operation and, one by one, he hauled three shells up to the gun, followed by three charges.

It was ten past three. Johnny opened the gun and heaved the first shell and charge into the breach. His hands smashed against the cold metal as he forced them in. Then he lit a cigarette, wiped sweat from his face and blood from his hands. The wind chilled the sweat on his back so he slipped his jacket on and sat by the gun.

He thought of KX4 and their chances of survival: held against the obvious results of the gunfire, those chances seemed pretty remote.

He also thought about Marieanne and the gunrunner he had yet to meet. Johnny felt an instinctive resentment towards Smith for being Marieanne's lover. Deep inside he nursed the constant fear that she would remarry and again reject him sexually. Her marriage had been the biggest blow he had ever taken. But the circumstances of their work made the logical remedy unthinkable, though it sometimes nagged the back of his mind and he would become conscious of the full extent of his selfishness — and hers.

He threw the cigarette away and looked down at the border post once more. It was nearly half past. He positioned himself at the gun, took aim, then watched the sweep hand of his Omega descend, hoping the gun was as efficient as it was clean.

It was. The gun recoiled from the shattering blast; Johnny stared down as the shell exploded just to the right of the post.

He rammed in the second shell and charge and re-adjusted his aim. Again the explosion echoed through the hills and he smiled at a mental picture of the guerrillas' panic. It had ripped into the centre of the sprawling post sending smoke and flames high into the air.

He was exhausted, his heart beat like a

piston engine as he prepared the gun for the last time. Again sweat ran down his chest and back, and his hands felt raw and painful. The shell obviously hit the ammunition store as a massive explosion lit up a wide area of the plain.

He didn't wait to see more. The Israelis' revenge would be swift and thorough. He ran to the Jeep, drove back down the steep track, and saw, reversing away from the caves, the truck El Dashiki's men had put the Lebanese drivers into. It turned at the bottom and sped across the flat area. Johnny sighed and reminded himself to lecture Marieanne on priorities as soon as he got the chance.

Then he drove towards the caves and pulled in behind some high rocks. He could hear the frightened babble of the Arabs; but then there was another sound — the increasing scream of jet aircraft.

* * *

Marieanne gripped Smith's wrist as the first shell was fired. The excitement outside the cave ceased immediately.

The second blast cut short the guerrillas' silence and their voices raised in fear. Footsteps ran along the corridor towards Smith and Marieanne. They pressed close to the wall.

The door burst open as the third shell fired and El Dashiki rushed in, followed by one of his officers. He was yelling something about Captain Jadid and the English spy, but, before they got to the desk, Marieanne stepped forward and Smith pushed the door to then locked it. The butt of her rifle smashed into the officer's neck and he fell to the ground unconscious. El Dashiki turned and his eyes stared in amazement at the girl and the gunrunner, then at the barrels of the two Israeli assault rifles.

'What have you done?' he rasped.

'Oh, we've just informed the Israelis of your presence. No doubt they will be paying us a visit soon — in their little French jets.'

The big Afro-Arab was too shocked by her reply to speak; he looked suspiciously at her airline bag and the holdall at Smith's feet.

'Yes, we have your money,' Marieanne told him. 'You didn't really intend to pay for the arms, did you? Now you've lost the lot.'

There was a knock at the door.

'Get rid of him,' she muttered. 'Tell him you'll be out soon — but no tricks.'

The knock became louder: urgent pleas for El Dashiki rang out above the other noise.

He hesitated then called out as ordered. The knocking and calls stopped.

'We'd better tie him up,' Smith suggested. 'There's some cord in that cupboard.'

Marieanne nodded:

'And the other one as well. We'll take them both.'

'Where is my Captain?' the guerrilla asked.

'Along the road somewhere. His jaw sort of got caught up with my friend's shoe so we left him searching for his teeth.'

Smith bound both men's hands behind their backs and Marieanne glanced at her watch: it was almost twenty to four.

Johnny would be on his way down from the hills. Any second would bring the inevitable retaliation.

'We'll never get out alive!' El Dashiki wailed. 'Mirages will smash these hills to pieces! You are fools — can't you see we will *all* die?'

Outside the office unheeded orders were being bellowed and screamed by the handful of officers and seniors. Rubber-soled feet stampeded in all directions.

Marieanne bit her lip.

'What are we waiting for?' Smith asked. She turned to him, her brow furrowed in thought for a few seconds before answering.

'If we go now we'll be stopped. But, if we wait until after the Israelis have made their first strike, we should be able to get out with no interference. By that time, I think, there will be a rather bad case of mass desertion.'

El Dashiki was sweating and his breath came in laboured sobs of fear.

Smith's optimism equalled that of the guerrilla, having long since convinced himself Marieanne was a suicidal maniac.

He felt close to death — and didn't like the feeling.

'What are you going to do with me?' the Arab asked.

'You're going to give us back our bacteria.'

She stood, feet apart, holding the nine-pound rifle as if it were a Woolworth's seven and elevenpenny toy.

'Oh no, Madame, even if we do get out of here I will never tell.'

Marieanne smiled. She had heard that one before.

Then the shouting and running stopped and one solitary voice wailed out a warning through the cave.

'The jets are coming,' she breathed.

'Jesus Christ!'

All Smith wanted to do then was drop his gun and light a cigarette: there seemed nothing to be gained by running. He looked at Marieanne's face: her eyes were bright and there was no fear — just excitement and a hint of wild pleasure. The little bitch was enjoying it all! Her gun was still trained on the guerrilla and she turned to Smith and grinned.

'Here they come, Hitchin: M.5 ground-attack Mirages, no doubt. And I bet each one is fully loaded with fourteen bombs.'

'Oh, goody!' Smith sneered. 'Can we go outside and watch?'

Then it sounded like the end of the world. The screaming jets swept overhead. Half the group seemed to be running into the cave; the other half seemed to want to get out. As the bombs spewed down there was a quick series of explosions; three of them shook the whole cave.

El Dashiki was demented: his lips moved but no sound came out. Then the jets roared into the distance.

Marieanne looked up:

'Now!'

Smith hauled the unconscious body over his shoulder and picked up the holdall.

The front of the cave had been hit; high piles of rocks partly blocked the entrance. Men were running in all directions; doors slammed, and nobody bothered to look at them. Bodies lay, bloody and broken, and odd limbs protruded from the fallen debris. Two trucks had been blasted and part of the arms and ammunition had gone up. They climbed over the rocks; Marieanne jabbed her rifle into El Dashiki's ribs as he hesitated and stumbled.

Some guerrillas had climbed into the remaining trucks and began to drive away. The first one was travelling too fast; it swerved, toppled over the side, and crashed on to the lower ground in a sheet of flame.

'Turn left and run!' Marieanne pointed down to where Johnny would be waiting.

The planes were returning and the Arabs desperately sought cover again. Marieanne was about ten yards behind Smith and El Dashiki, covering in case a rescue was attempted. But, as no one seemed to care about their beloved leader any more, she turned and ran towards the others.

Johnny sprinted up to Smith and pulled the officer from his shoulder. Smith spun round, yelling at Marieanne to hurry. He saw two men run from the cave; one raised his rifle at her.

'Watch out!'

She fell flat as the Arab fired and Smith's shots were drowned by the Mirages' attack. He got both of them and, in the same second, a bomb dropped in front of the cave. Both bodies were blasted into the air.

Marieanne raised her hands against the flying debris and ran towards the Jeep. Sudden pain seered into the back of her left thigh and something rough and heavy smashed against her shoulder. But she carried on.

'Have you got the money?' Johnny held her arms.

She nodded.

'Good — get in.' He almost threw her into the Jeep then ran to the front.

Smith sat beside her and El Dashiki was pushed down opposite. She said nothing but was conscious of pain and the warm dampness of flowing blood. Something was embedded in her leg and every movement was agony. Her shoulder felt raw and bruised.

Then they were speeding down from the hills. Two of the fleeing lorries had been hit by the second attack: they burned away on the flat ground where the freedom fighters had trained daily for their glorious attack and victory over the Jews. Bodies had been thrown out and some were burning.

The Mirages returned for a third attack but restricted themselves to the hills. El Dashiki stared back at the destruction of all his hopes and dreams.

* * *

After a while Johnny stopped and jumped lightly into the back. Smith leaned forward and looked at him closely for the first time. So, this was Marieanne's side-kick, underling, superior, or what have you. He certainly wasn't what he had expected.

'Hitchin Smith, I presume. My name's Armstrong — Johnny Armstrong.'

'I suppose you're the bloody fool who fired the gun. Don't know whether I should be pleased to meet you or not.' But Smith smiled as he took the extended hand.

'Still, I suppose it got us out of that place. Do you two do this sort of thing often?'

'Oh, we can cause quite a stir — on occasions.' Johnny raised a hand to his head and slender fingers carefully smoothed the windblown waves.

Daylight had broken into the darkness. The officer was regaining consciousness and began to groan and writhe about the floor.

Johnny was still being surveyed closely. He had an interesting face, Smith decided — maybe a little effeminate but undeniably attractive. It was also rather grimy. His voice was precise and accentless — a perfect match for his appearance. By then Smith had discounted all his earlier thoughts and fears on Marieanne's relationship with her colleague: he was convinced this long-locked agent with the big, dreamy eyes and mannerisms of a ballet dancer, was as camp as a row of tents.

Johnny turned to El Dashiki.

'Hello, happy. You look as if you've lost a couple of million and found a piastre

— or was it a disaster?'

The guerrilla glared up at him then shut his eyes.

The other Arab struggled into a sitting position but Johnny knocked him back with a blow to the neck. Then he held his hand, looked at it closely, and turned to Smith.

'Would you mind driving, Hitchin? I scraped my hands on that gun.' He held them out, exposing the gashes and oily dirt.

Smith handed him the assault rifle and climbed over into the driver's seat. He turned, looked at Johnny again, then shrugged.

'Anywhere in particular?'

'To your plane, lover. Then we fly to wherever this rat has hidden the bacteria.'

'My bloody plane won't go.' He drove on.

'I think it will — when *we* get there.'

Smith sighed. No doubt his plane *would* go when *they* got there.

'I take it I'm dealing with two smart-arses now?'

Johnny laughed.

'Something like that.'

He turned to Marieanne and began to berate her for freeing the Lebanese drivers. She refused to look at him.

'They would have been killed,' she argued. 'Anyway, it's done now and cost us nothing.'

'That's not the . . . '

'Oh, shut up, Johnny!' She closed her eyes and leaned back. Although cold and shivery, she had to wipe sweat from her forehead.

He leaned close.

'Are you all right, Marieanne? You're as pale as death.'

'I'm tired and hungry — that's all.'

8

Hens, ducks and dogs scattered as the Jeep sped past villages and homesteads. Goats ceased their incessant munching to stare and, at occasional windows, sleepless faces surveyed the disturbance of their peace. Interruptions had become a routine in that part of the country: Israelis frequently raided villages; homes would be damaged, even burnt to the ground; guerrillas or hostages would be captured. Then, in vain, half-hearted attempts to weed out terrorists, Lebanese army patrols would swoop down.

'There's no need to kill us,' Johnny called. 'Slow down — nobody's after us.'

'I'm taking no chances,' Smith shouted back. 'We can't be all that popular with El Dashiki's men.'

'They won't bother us again. The last person they want to be near now is their trusty leader.'

Despite Johnny's assurances, Smith

kept his foot hard down. They jolted over stones, down potholes, through gritty dustpools. Marieanne held the side, wincing as the seat lurched against her leg. Conversation and comfort were impossible; it seemed an eternity before Smith swung into the airfield, roared over to the plane and braked at the last moment. The back of the Jeep swung round, almost flinging Johnny and Marieanne on to the Arabs' knees.

'Oh, for Christ's sake,' Johnny complained. 'You don't have to run into the bloody thing! We've got to fly to Beirut in it.'

Smith jumped down and ran to the front of the Cessna.

There was no sign of Ali.

'Ali! . . . Ali, you bastard! Where the hell are you?'

There was no reply. He turned to the others.

'Maybe he's gone to stretch his legs,' Johnny suggested.

'I'll stretch his bloody neck!' Smith snapped. 'He's probably fled into the hills. They're all the same these Arabs.

Wait till I catch up with him — he won't know whether his arse's been bored or punched!'

Then he noticed the message fastened to the pilot's door and walked up to it. It stated in Ali's unique written English : —

'Gon to Beirut for spares as some wyring and attatshments missing. All spare wyr gon as well. Downt understand.'

Marieanne peered over his shoulder.

'What does it say?'

He read it out loud then went on:

'No wonder he doesn't blasted understand — neither do I!'

'He should have waited. There was no need for him to go off like that. I left them there.' She pointed towards the crumbling building.

Smith turned to her, visibly shocked.

'My God, you scheming little bitch! I should have known. You never intended any of us to get back to Beirut until you'd completed your mission.'

'Well, go on, get them,' she urged. 'They're under that windowsill. I put them there just before I shot our three visitors.'

Smith shoved his hands deep into his back pockets and strode over to the wall, returning with the length of cable and its end attachments. Then he fiddled in the engine, cursing everybody concerned, the bad light, and the situation in general. Finally he climbed into the pilot's seat and the Cessna burst into healthy life. He taxied down the scrubby runway and, for a moment, Marieanne wondered if he would take off and leave them. But the plane turned, its lights shining out as he came alongside.

She opened the passenger door; the two Arabs were pushed down to the back and Johnny retied their feet. Marieanne walked up front and sat beside Smith.

'I take it you know a bit about planes?' he asked.

'Oh yes, we've both got pilot's licences.'

'That figures!' He glanced over his shoulder. 'What are we bringing the other Arab along with us for?'

'Obviously you know less about Arabs than we do,' she answered. 'They're often reluctant to talk unless an example is made — then their tongues loosen quite rapidly.'

'You've come across this sort of thing before?'

'Often.'

He shook his head.

'You're certainly a charming pair — you and that bloody fairy friend of yours.'

Johnny called from the back:

'Do you mind cutting out the chat and getting this thing off the ground?'

Smith checked the controls quickly and strapped himself in. Five minutes later they were in the air and heading north. Marieanne watched him closely — he was a good pilot.

Johnny crouched in front of El Dashiki, smiling benignly at him.

'Well now, we seem to be alone here — away from all that nasty confusion below. I think it's about time we got down to business, don't you? You seem a bright kind of chap to me — underneath all that dirt — and realise why you're here, I suppose. We want our KX4 back. It's an extremely potent and dangerous weapon.

We can't allow Arabs to run around with things like that. Let's face it, lover, nobody minds you sons of the desert leaping about in flowing robes, on camels, shooting at one another; but when it comes to wiping out whole nations — well, it's not very nice, is it? I don't think Allah would like it one little bit.'

El Dashiki's face remained impassive.

'You will never get it back,' he said calmly, 'No matter what you do to me. I have already made arrangements as to its disposal; it will pass into the hands of others like me.'

'But that won't do *you* much good, will it? I thought you wanted to get to the top — the leader of Arab victory and all that crap. There's no glory in dying *this* way.'

Johnny paused. El Dashiki said nothing so he went on:

'We realised that you might be a little unco-operative at first and that's why we've brought your friend along. Of course I could be foolish and take you at your first word, in which case you'd be tossed out here and now, but it wouldn't be much good for either of us if you

189

changed your mind on the way down. Just think how disappointed we'd both be when we couldn't bring you back to listen. And you'd die. So, what we've decided to do, in order to persuade you to change your mind *before* resorting to violence on *your* person is to throw your friend out — sort of a preview of what will happen to you if you won't talk.'

'And if I do talk, what guarantee will you give that I will live?'

'You'll have to take a gamble and trust us — put it down to our deep gratitude for the information you have imparted.'

'I will impart nothing!'

Johnny moved down the plane and opened the floor cargo hatch. A blast of cold air rushed in.

'You would not do such a thing,' El Dashiki called. 'Why kill him? He knows nothing.'

'I don't doubt he knows nothing, baby, but we mean business and, unfortunately for him, your mate is the pawn in our game.'

The other Arab stared round in horror, desperately seeking a way out of his hopeless situation. Then he started to wail out for his leader to save him. But El Dashiki leaned back against the side of the plane and turned his head away from his officer as Johnny returned. Tears started to roll down the victim's cheeks; he started to scream for help. He wasn't a young man; fear trembled through his thin body and sweat rolled down the quivering nose into his moustache.

'He's not going to chuck that poor sod out, is he?' Smith demanded.

Marieanne turned and smiled vaguely.

'Wait and see.'

'You're both sick — psychopathic killers.'

'Just keep on a straight course to Beirut, Hitchin.' She eased herself out of the seat. 'Johnny and I will worry about the rest.'

She moved slowly and carefully down the plane.

The condemned man's eyes were wide with terror; she'd never seen so much white in two eyes. His sobbed pleas had diminished into no more than whispers and he shrank back as Johnny held his ankles. Together they dragged him forward. He screamed and struggled; Smith closed his eyes as the body dropped into space and the yells were lost.

Marieanne and Johnny went back to El Dashiki. The first shadows of fear had appeared on his face. He started to speak but the words were lost in stammers.

'We'll find KX4 whether you talk or not,' Johnny told him. 'We know the kind of place it will have to be stored in, and will search every laboratory, clinic, hospital, and university, etcetera, until we find it. But it would help immensely if you co-operated. I hate searching around places — it's such a waste of time.' His voice was relaxed and soothing.

Marieanne knelt beside him.

'Come on and talk,' she urged. 'This is your last chance.'

He had lost most of his composure but his eyes were still defiant and he remained silent. Johnny shook his head slowly, looked at the palms of his hands and rubbed his fingers lightly over the grazes.

'Are you going to insist on being foolish about all this?'

Still nothing.

'Well, I'm afraid we're not prepared to wait any longer.'

He grabbed the Arab's feet and hauled him up towards the open hatch where Marieanne guided the writhing head and shoulders over the opening.

'You'd better talk,' Johnny advised. 'It's hard down there — bad for the bones.'

El Dashiki was pushed further over the hatchway; beads of sweat formed on his face and were blown over it by the air current.

'Talk, for Christ's sake!' Smith shouted. 'If I were you I'd recite the blasted Koran backwards!'

Every second the Arab was slipping further and further out into oblivion. He'd had enough.

'I'll talk!' he wailed. 'I'll tell you all you want to know, but pull me back!'

But he was left there for another minute before being dragged back to safety. Hysterical sobs overcame him and he cowered away from them.

'That's better,' Johnny began. 'I knew you'd eventually see the light. I've got a way with people, haven't I, Marieanne? At first they don't like me but, sooner or later, they all come round . . . '

'Cut out the gloating,' Marieanne snapped. 'And shut the hatch — it's freezing in here.' Johnny's cat-and-mouse tactics irritated her.

He slammed the hatch then crouched beside her. El Dashiki was still in no shape to talk coherently.

Then Johnny saw the injury; he straightened her leg and looked closely at the wound, but it was impossible to see clearly under the torn denim: the back of her jeans was a mass of coagulated and fresh blood — it had even soaked her sock and run into her shoe.

'A bullet?' he asked.

She shook her head and told him how it had happened.

'Don't move — stay absolutely still, love, then the bleeding will ease off.' His hand gripped her knee and he gave a parental 'be brave' smile. 'I'll see to you as soon as we get to Beirut.'

For a few seconds her hand closed tightly over his before he turned back to their prisoner, who had stopped sobbing and moaning.

'Now then, Mr Dashiki, I hope you weren't having me on and we won't have to go through the whole painful procedure again. I'm afraid I wouldn't listen to you any more — you'd just be tipped out.'

'Where is KX4?' asked Marieanne.

'In Aley,' he muttered.

'Where in Aley?'

'Rue Saliba . . . There is a private clinic — La Clinique Emir Bechir . . . Your bacteria is there. I'll take you to it.' Tears flooded his eyes and merged into the sweat by his fat nose.

Johnny gave a dramatic sigh of relief.

'Now isn't that nice of him, Marieanne? He's going to take us there himself. I always said Arabs only need the right kind of treatment then they'll give you the world.' He grinned smugly at the dejected black face. 'Yes, I can see it now; we'll all four walk up to the clinic; El Dashiki will knock on the door; we'll be invited in and each have a glass of arak and a pleasant chat. Then we'll collect our germs, pack them into a suitcase and take them back to England, or put them on the next plane to Australia.'

'Then what will you do with me?' El Dashiki asked.

'Oh, we won't be interested in you any more: you can go back to terrorising Jews if you want to. Mrs Payne and I will go back to London to our respective cosy little flats, and Mr Smith will . . . ' He stood up, leaned over the passenger seat, and raised his voice. ' . . . Well, Mr Smith hasn't exactly covered himself with glory from a gunrunning point of view. His way of life has sort of been upset, to say the least. I think he's lost a customer.'

Smith had an almost uncontrollable urge to rush down the plane and smash Armstrong. It seemed to him that he was the only one to have lost out on the deal: it wasn't a question of money — he still stood to make his cut — but he'd lost face and, most probably, his reputation. He doubted whether El Dashiki would live to spread the word, but there were some survivors from the guerrilla group.

'Marieanne,' he began tartly, 'tell your

lovely man friend to keep his big, sarcastic mouth shut for a few minutes — that is, if he can: we're coming in to land.'

★   ★   ★

Ali ran from the office to meet them. Johnny pushed El Dashiki out and Smith helped Marieanne down. The Iraqi's voice was shrill with excitement and surprise; he danced around the ground, nodding and smiling at everyone.

'How did you get away?' he finally asked Smith. 'Didn't you notice that part of the wiring was missing?'

'Of course I bloody well noticed that part of the wiring was missing. Your much-admired El Sitt had removed it while we slept. How do you think we got here — with an elastic band?'

Ali surveyed Marieanne for a moment then shrugged.

'But how was I to know, Mr Smith? I had to come back to get the replacements. They couldn't guarantee to get them down to Sour before weekend.'

Smith was exhausted.

'Just stop asking questions and go and get us something to eat, on the double. We're hungry. El Dashiki wasn't exactly abounding in typical Arabic hospitality: not even one sheep's eye all the time we were there.'

Ali stuck out his hand; Smith slapped a wad of Lebanese pounds into it.

Before leaving he had another look at the little group; he was still reeling at the sudden turn of events. Armstrong was no stranger to Ali. He had driven up to him two days before, identifying himself as a tourist. They had spent a lazy hour in the sun, their conversation flowing from the sorry state of the Middle East and the cursed Jews, to the profits of hashish smuggling. Now he had turned up again with Smith, El Sitt, and their customer who, from appearances, had not been willing or able to pay for his arms.

The presence of this captive saddened Ali: he admired all freedom fighters — their leaders were his heroes. However, his Arab nationalism had tempered to limitations since meeting Hitchin Smith and his first loyalties now lay with the tall, black-haired Englishman who had made all things possible for him. Smith's enemies were Ali's enemies — regardless of whether they were dedicated to smashing the Jews or not.

It was all very confusing but, as Smith appeared to be in bad humour, he didn't press for explanations though burning with curiosity.

'Is there anything special Ma'mseille Lessard would like?' His face beamed and he rubbed his hands together. He felt no anger towards her for incapacitating his plane — she must have had her reasons.

'Oh, by the way,' Smith cut in, 'it's Mrs Payne now.'

Ali looked puzzled and muttered, 'Payne?'

'Yes, Payne — like in the arse.' He waved his hand towards Johnny. 'And this is Mr Armstrong. I should keep your back to the wall while he's around.'

★   ★   ★

199

While Ali was gathering provisions in Jdaidé, Johnny took the medical kit from the plane and dealt with Marieanne's injuries. The bruising and broken skin on her shoulder was cleaned and covered with a thick pad of lint plastered to her back. Then he cut the stiff, gory jeans from her leg and washed away the blood. After inspection and swabbing he saw the cause of the trouble and carefully extracted a fragment of shell. The injury wasn't as serious as it might have been but needed stitching, as Smith repeatedly pointed out. His suggestion that a doctor or hospital should be visited was turned down: she would have to wait until the job was done, then she could have stitches from head to foot, if she wanted.

Afterwards she changed into a moss-green shirtwaister. The holster underneath pressed painfully against her shoulder and the bulky dressing on her thigh protruded from under the short skirt.

Ali arrived burdened with food and wine which he spread over the table. They washed the dust and grime off themselves then ate in silence: sesame bread dipped in hommus; tabboule salad eaten with a communal spoon — the only one they had, and long, hot shishkebab.

El Dashiki's wrists had been freed. Despite his degradation he ate heartily, continually wiping his mouth on the dirty tunic and glancing across the table at the Luger by Johnny's hand.

After the meal Johnny paced around the office, stopping each time he passed the dull mirror to arrange his thick, sun-streaked hair. His hands were covered in small bandaids and he had discarded the blood-stained jacket. Smith watched him; he was light-footed and prowled round in studious rumination, occasionally looking up at one or the other of them. His eyes revealed no tiredness.

Smith leaned back against the table, his eyes heavy with lack of sleep.

'What would have happened if he hadn't talked?' he yawned.

Johnny spun round.

'He would have bitten the dust, I can assure you. It's also possible that the end would have been in sight for a large proportion of the Israeli population: whether that would be a good or a bad thing depends entirely upon one's personal convictions. I never really held out much hope of finding the germs without his help.'

He took El Dashiki into the other room, pushed him on to the bunk and rebound him securely before walking back to the others.

'Go and guard him.' He threw the Luger over to Ali, who caught it, stared down at it in awe, then shuffled through, slamming the door behind him.

'How can you be sure the Israelis haven't already helped themselves to your precious bugs?' Smith demanded. 'If they can run off with a ten-ton radar station right from under the Arabs' noses a little case of germs shouldn't present much of a problem.'

'I can't be sure, but wherever KX4 is, my love, we have to get it back.'

'We?' Smith demanded. 'I've carried out my part of the bargain, Armstrong, and plenty more besides. I'm getting the first plane back to London. If you think

I'm going to start chasing around Israel for bugs — which we just might have to do — you're sadly mistaken. The Jews are a damn sight more clever than the Arabs. It was nothing short of a miracle that we got out of El Dashiki's camp — I'm not going to trust my luck a second time.'

There was silence for a moment and Smith waited in vain for the reaction he expected. He turned to Marieanne: she was smoking a suspicious-smelling cigarette Ali had given her — one of his customers' samples — and drinking from a large tumbler of wine. Her face registered contented drowsiness; the abundant hair fell over her shoulders and her dress was unbuttoned low. She looked up at Johnny, smiled faintly, then leaned forward, reconcentrating her gaze on the smoke that rose from her cigarette.

'There's nothing you two can do to keep me here,' Smith stated, completely knocked off balance by the nil reception his declaration had received.

Johnny shrugged; his eyebrows shot towards the carefully arranged hair in apparent unconcern.

'Of course there isn't, Hitchin. You shouldn't have any difficulty getting out of the country. I don't suppose the army or police are looking for you in connection with all the bodies they've found over the last forty-eight hours — not yet anyway.'

Smith looked up at him; the emphasis on the last three words translated only too clearly.

'And what good would it do you if you dropped me in the cart?'

'Oh, it wouldn't do us any good at all, Hitchin baby, but it would do us a great deal of good if you were to forget all these silly ideas about rushing back to London and stay here to help us. However, if you insist on leaving, then I might get overcome with good citizenship and tell the authorities all I know — with plenty of embroidery, of course.'

Smith laughed bitterly.

'Not only are you a murdering bastard, Armstrong — you're also a rotten, blackmailing little queer!'

He rose from his chair and stood in

front of Johnny, who reacted to the insults by smiling and pulling a long strand of hair down over his ear.

'O.K., so I stay,' he went on. 'But, before we go any further with the deal, I'm going to get some deep and personal satisfaction out of smashing you right in the mouth.'

Marieanne looked up in vague and dreamy interest as Smith's fist drew back. But it was one of his more inaccurate calculations. The blow was deflected upwards; history repeated itself and he somersaulted once, smashing against the opposite door, which burst open, and landed on his back at Ali's feet. Ali immediately proved his quick reflexes and value as a guard by dropping his gun and raising his hands high. But the fear soon turned to a snigger when he realised what had happened and he helped his partner up. Smith swore at him then limped back into the other room.

'You've ruined me between the two of you,' he stated, and swung round to Marieanne expecting some little sign of sympathy. She gazed blankly from one to the other, continued her wine and drew deeply on the cigarette. Then she closed her eyes.

'So what?' Johnny asked. 'I heard a rumour that you were thinking of retiring from gunrunning.'

'The thought had crossed my mind.'

'And what pastimes have you mapped out for this early retirement?' Marieanne asked sleepily. 'I can't really picture you with a chicken farm or shooting grouse on the moors. Where would you get your kicks from?'

'Don't either of you worry about me — kicks are easily found.'

Johnny threw him a cigarette.

'If you were to tie in with us you'd never be short of excitement — of one kind or another.' He inclined his head towards Marieanne.

'Tie in with you two?' Smith exclaimed. 'My God, it'd be like working with Dr Crippen and Jack the Ripper!'

'Now you're exaggerating, Hitchin. I doubt very much that such thoughts crossed your mind when you were making love to my beautiful colleague.'

Both men were silent. Marieanne was asleep in the big, battered swivel chair where Ali usually plotted the courses of his smuggling deals. Exhaustion, wine, and Ali's special blend had overcome her.

'Your gunrunning will be a terrific cover,' Johnny went on; 'far more original than the outplayed diplomatic courier.'

'After this, my gunrunning days will probably be numbered.'

'No they won't — *if* you are wise. We'll see to it that you retain your reputation. You're a highly respected man — just the type we want.' Johnny's voice had lost all its former cynicism.

Smith said no more. For a moment he looked at Johnny then walked into the other room. He turned Ali and El Dashiki out then lay on the bunk. He was tired, so tired he found it difficult to wrestle with the troublesome thoughts bogging him down.

As he saw it he had two alternatives. He could leave Beirut and, if Johnny was bluffing, go back to England. But he didn't think Johnny was bluffing, and pictured himself being ignominiously dragged from a B.O.A.C. Boeing by the army or the police: an extremely unattractive thought. Gaol in Beirut was another prospect looming ahead — even more unattractive.

He could carry on, of course, until the job was done. The worst part was over — or so he hoped. If he did stay with them Smith knew there would be no trouble with the authorities — for any of them.

He hadn't liked Armstrong from the instant he had first met him, but admired the way he went about his work. To say the least, he knew what he was doing, and did it efficiently and successfully. My God, he thought, what a formidable pair they are!

With that final thought Smith decided to stay. Once back in London he'd hot-foot it away — far, far away.

The door opened; Johnny walked in carrying Marieanne.

'Move over,' he said softly, then laid her down beside him.

'How long have you worked together?'

'About nine years,' Johnny answered.

'Christ, you must have charmed lives.

Did you meet up through your work?'

He shook his head.

'No, I knew Marieanne for a while before we started training.' He hesitated and looked intently at Smith, who didn't fail to notice the hint of pain in the clear, green eyes. 'We were no more than kids then ... ' He sighed. 'She was only eighteen ... '

Smith wanted to ask more but Johnny cut him short.

'Get some sleep. You need it. I doubt that we'll get any tonight.'

He left the room quickly and Smith gazed down at Marieanne. It seemed inconceivable that she could have been embroiled in such a way of life for nine years. Her face was peaceful in sleep and he ran his hand over her cool forehead. All the hate he'd worked up for her in El Dashiki's cell was forgotten. He lay back and she turned and curled towards him in sleep. He eased her bandaged leg over his and slid his arms round her. Her steady breathing was soon lulling him to sleep and he held her close, conscious of the revolver sandwiched between their ribs.

9

Smith awoke to the smell of food. Marieanne was no longer with him and it was dark. For a while he lay on his back, listening to the voices from the other room. Ali was babbling away excitedly with the others in a mixture of French and Arabic. Eventually curiosity overtook him; he changed into white jeans and a pink denim shirt, then walked through.

Ali was opening packages of food again, spreading them out carelessly on the table where Marieanne and Johnny sat together, closely examining a piece of paper. El Dashiki had obviously been making a nuisance of himself — he was gagged and no place had been made for him at the table.

As they ate Johnny pushed the paper across to Smith.

'Voilá — la Clinique Emir Bechir,' he announced.

Smith turned the paper round and

looked at the meticulously detailed drawing.

'While you two beauties were sleeping I was busy — everything's organised.'

'Good for you,' Smith commented, then glanced over the table; a furrow of consternation appeared across his forehead. 'How come there's no wine, Ali, and where's my arak?'

Ali shrugged and pointed at Johnny, who answered for him:

'No alcohol tonight, Hitchin — or hash. We need all our wits and quick reactions.'

Smith muttered inaudibly then slapped another heap of tabboule on to his plate in disgust before cutting viciously into a large piece of grilled lamb.

'The first thing I did,' Johnny went on. 'Was to get a car — one that won't advertise our presence as much as Ali's crate of many colours. Then, as you will have realised, I drove to Aley and made a quick survey of the clinic.'

His finger traced over the sketch as he described what he had seen:

Rue Saliba ran along one of the many

hills surrounding Aley. The villas were built on a steep slope. At the back of the clinic the pine-covered hill rose steeply. The grounds at the front and sides of the clinic were surrounded by a high wall topped with a narrow wrought-iron trimming. There were no grounds at the rear — the wall slanted in to the back of the clinic. The entire back of the building had had all the doors and windows completely bricked up.

'As you can see, there's no possible way of getting in from the back,' Johnny explained. 'There doesn't appear to be anything unusual about the front of the place. Because of the steep slope the building is split-level — two storeyed at the front; one at the back. The wrought-iron on the wall is, I am certain, rigged with warning devices.'

He sat back and looked around the room: El Dashiki remained hungry in his silent world of gagged and sullen depression, his big, marbly eyes staring across at them. Smith appeared to be testing how far he could lean back in his chair without it falling. Ali sat on the floor against the filing cabinet, Johnny's Luger in one hand, a tall glass of fruit juice in the other. El Dashiki turned and stared longingly at the drink and Ali taunted him by tinkling the ice cubes together.

Ali had had a hard day and wasn't feeling quite so warmly disposed towards this new Englishman. Johnny had kept him on the go — he had to collect the car from the city, fetch lunch, then guard El Dashiki while Johnny was gone for two hours in the afternoon. They had been two nerve-wracking, fear-filled hours for the Iraqi. Every sound had either been a platoon of vengeful Israelis or a group of enraged Arab terrorists. Every change in expression on El Dashiki's black face was the reflection of plans for foolproof escape — and death for him.

'Well, what else?' Smith demanded. 'Surely you didn't go to all that trouble just to look at a few walls?'

'There wasn't much else I could do, love, except for one little thing.' He turned back to their prisoner.

'I know you've changed your attitude about things, Mr Dashiki, but, just in case you and your mates at the clinic decide to have one last fling, I've planted an effective amount of plastic explosive under the back wall.' He pulled a small, squat timing device from his pocket. 'One flick of the switch and puff — no more clinic. So, for your own and everybody else's sakes, don't give us any more trouble.'

El Dashiki swallowed nervously and nodded. Smith could again do no more than admire Johnny's efficiency.

* * *

They left at eight o'clock. Ali's troubles weren't over as, instead of driving home to the warm bosom of his plump wife and large family, he was unanimously chosen to accompany them — to be at the wheel of the car ready for the getaway.

He sat in the back of the sleek black Pontiac with Johnny. El Dashiki had been pushed on to the floor — they had used him as a footrest.

Marieanne sat up front with Smith, who negotiated the crazy traffic with a

214

casual abandon that could only be achieved by long experience.

He knew Beirut and surrounding districts like the proverbial back of his hand. By choice it had become the centre of his business; he had developed a deep affection for the whole country and its exuberant, cosmopolitan people. He proved his liking by returning the fist waving and loud abuse, so important to Lebanese driving.

There was no need to re-enter the city centre: he took the road south out of Jdaidé, past the quarters of sleezy Borj Hammoud and Sin El Fil; through the pine woods, then over the river on to the Damascus road. They ran the gauntlet with countless service taxis — the 'voitures de service' that circle the city and travel to the resort towns — even as far as Damascus.

* * *

Aley stands on a hill twenty-two miles from Beirut, overlooking the capital and a great stretch of the coastline that, at night, stretches out in the distance like a long necklace of lights.

The pine-blanketed hills around the small town are shady hideaways for the villas of the wealthy; casinos and parklands. The casinos and star-crusted hotels were well known to Smith: he spent many hours in them — spending, losing and winning.

As they drove towards the town, a thick sprinkling of lights sparkled out through the trees leaving no division between the hills and starlit sky.

Rue Saliba was on the far side of Aley. Johnny gave Smith directions, eventually telling him to pull in off the road. The car came to a halt beneath a large overhanging tree.

'It's about fifty yards further on,' Johnny said. 'Ali can wait for us here.'

Smith twisted round and stuck his finger in Ali's chest.

'Now listen; as soon as you see us come out of that gate — be ready. So keep awake.' He leaned over and grabbed the Iraqi by the front of his white shirt. 'If we come running out of there with an army of Arabs after us and you're asleep behind this wheel, so help me, I'll punch you so hard in the mouth, next time you want to bite your nails you'll have to stick your fingers up your arse!'

Johnny replaced Marieanne's small revolver with a Luger and handed Smith a sub-machine gun.

'That should be more in your line,' he told him. 'You ought to be an expert after all the demonstrations you've given over the years.'

Then he untied El Dashiki and ordered him out of the car. The others followed and Ali climbed over into the driver's seat.

For a moment they stood in the cool night air. Marieanne bent her leg a few times — it had stiffened during the journey. Ali leaned out of the window and fervently wished Allah's presence on them, feeling quite grateful for his background role in the operation. He leaned on the wheel and watched them walk away; Smith and Johnny flanked the Arab closely; Marieanne turned once and waved her hand.

The superb villas were partly buried behind thick bushes, trees and tall hedges. In the daytime flowers blazed a kaleidoscope of colour over the rich greenness: at night porch lights, and the floodlights of the very rich, accentuated the darkness of the unlit road.

One side of the hill loomed high and black behind the villas and trees; over the roofs and trees on the other side they could see across to the winking lights on other hills.

A gleaming white Mercedes swung in front of them and whispered through a gateway, up towards the near-palace beyond. The whole road epitomised the affluence of the area.

They reached the clinic and Smith took a small flashlight from his pocket which he shone up on to the plaque set in the high wall: apart from the name of the clinic there was nothing else except one green embossed cedar. The tall gates were elaborate black wrought iron.

'I presume you know how to get in without setting of all the bells, chimes and sirens,' Marieanne asked El Dashiki. He nodded and crouched down; his hand slid under the edge of the gate. There was the click of a switch. He stood up and handed a key to Johnny.

'You can unlock the gates now,' he muttered. 'Nothing will happen.'

'Thank you,' Johnny said cheerfully. 'You're quite a decent fellow, considering. I might even buy you a drink when all this is over.'

He unlocked the gate and they walked on to the tiled driveway.

'I suppose I'd be right in assuming this place is run solely for the benefit of terrorist organisations?' Marieanne whispered.

'Yes, the patients consist entirely of injured guerrillas.'

Smith wanted to laugh for the first time in days.

'Injured guerrillas?' he echoed. 'Fell out of their bloody banana trees, I suppose.'

The driveway was long and so steep it reduced them to breathlessness. Tall, closely packed conifers flanked both sides. Finally they had passed the last curve and the flat-roofed clinic was straight ahead. As Johnny had said it was two storeyed at the front; two deep loggias ran along the full width of the building; the upper one had a wrought-iron rail from which vines and creeping plants tumbled down over the five pointed arches of the bottom loggia.

The centre arch and front entrance were reached by three wide steps edged with pots of bright red flowered plants. A light flooded down from above the dark solid wooden door. The windows were covered with ornamental, but strong, grilles; light slid out thinly from under the blinds of those on either side of the door. The loggia was full of flowers — in tubs, boxes, and pots; the perfume from them hung heavily in the air, and cicadas and other night creatures sang out happily.

They walked quietly up the steps. Marieanne pulled Smith back from the door and they pressed against the wall. Johnny nodded and El Dashiki knocked.

A small grille opened, emitting a square of bright light. An eye peered out then an excited voice called El Dashiki's name. A couple of heavy bolts were drawn; a key turned. As the door opened, Johnny darted forward and threw his full weight against it. It smashed against the guard's head and he fell to the floor, unconscious.

Two other guards sat on either side of the stairs which led from the centre of the hall. They jumped to their feet but the second's hesitation was enough for Smith to fire a quick burst between them before they could reach for their rifles. They froze; Marieanne pushed El Dashiki over to them, picked up the rifles which she emptied then dropped. She flung the ammunition under a tall cabinet.

A door opened and a slim, balding man in a grey suit peered around it. Johnny sprang forward and dragged him over to the guards.

'Your name?' he asked in French.

'Dr Khoury — Hamoud Khoury. What is all this?'

'Are you in charge here?'

'Yes — this is my clinic. Who are you?'

His questions were ignored and Marieanne asked:

'Who else is here?'

The doctor hesitated until becoming

too conscious of the Lugers and sub-machine gun.

'Just two nurses and three patients.'

'Where?'

He pointed to the door he had been pulled through.

'Upstairs?' Johnny demanded.

'There is no one up there — it is just the staff's quarters.'

'Check every room,' he told Marieanne. 'Bring anyone you find here.'

She came back with two young and very frightened nurses, who took their places with the doctor.

'The patients won't bother us,' she explained. 'They're obviously survivors from a border raid; two are on drips and the third is mummified in bandages.'

Dr Khoury began to protest that his patients required constant care.

'Where's your laboratory?' Johnny asked.

'Why — what do you want with the laboratory?' His eyes registered a fresh wave of alarm and he turned to El Dashiki. 'Who are these people?'

But the black Arab didn't reply; he just

sighed noisily through his teeth and concentrated on the intricate ceiling pattern.

'We want the bacteria he gave you to look after,' Marieanne told him.

Apart from having the explosive pointed out to him, little more persuasion was needed. The doctor pointed to a door on the opposite side of the hall.

It didn't take Marieanne long to discover the flex running from a wall socket into a padlocked cupboard, which she wrenched open with a retort stand. She unplugged the lead from the base of the fat, stainless-steel canister and lifted it by the plastic-clad handle. It was heavy — at least twenty-five pounds. The storage elements would retain heat for hours.

El Dashiki's despair reached its lowest ebb when she returned to the hall with the canister.

'Well, that seems to be that,' Johnny smiled. 'Now we can take our little picnic flask back home.'

'No.'

Both he and Smith stared at her.

'It's not going back to England — nor to Australia. I'm going to get rid of it before something else happens.'

'But that wasn't the Master's idea, darling. They consider those germs to be extremely valuable and they want them back.'

'We might not be able to get them back a second time, Johnny. Besides, if they bred this lot they'll soon produce more.'

Smith saw the stubbornness he'd seen so many times before but was inclined to agree with her, and said so. Johnny nodded his head slowly.

'O.K. then, get rid of them. But you'd better think of some real good story to cover their loss.'

'There must be some sort of incinerator here,' she said, then addressed Khoury. 'Where?'

'Through the door next to the laboratory.'

The door opened on to a flight of stairs; at the bottom two doors faced one another. She found the right one first and stepped inside. The dry, hot air of the room irritated her nose and throat.

224

Opposite stood an oil-fed boiler and the incinerator. She walked across to it, pulled the flap open — a blast of seering heat swept upwards. Then she knelt, slipped the cumbersome gun into her holster, and began to unscrew the top of the canister. The inside was no more than two inches in diameter; she pulled it directly under the light. The contents appeared to be housed in a plastic cyclinder that would, she hoped, slide down without having to touch it. The dark, nutritive jelly clung patchily to the top of the inner container.

Again she lifted the canister and crossed over to the incinerator.

'Put that down and turn round!' Her hand was on the flap. She did as bid. Two young men walked towards her from the other room; each held a revolver.

'Your gun, please.' The smaller man took the Luger from her holster and stuck it down his belt.

'We knew you would do the job for us — we only had to wait.' He smiled triumphantly then spoke in Hebrew to the other man, who took the canister and screwed the lid back on. He was tall, pale and fair haired: a very un-Jewish Jew.

'With possession of these we can make the Arabs behave themselves.' His English was accentless.

'Unfortunately,' the first one began, 'the only way out of here is past your friends, and our mutual enemies. So, until we are safely away, you will remain with us.'

Marieanne looked at them; the bright and unmistakable light of Israeli militaristic chauvinism burned in their eyes. She wondered how the two clever bastards had managed to get into the clinic unnoticed.

They signalled her to walk in front; a gun was only inches from her spine.

Smith became more uneasy every second Marieanne was away. His sub-machine gun covered the assortment of guards, nurses, and the doctor. The guard who had been knocked for six was conscious; he slouched against the wall holding his head. Continually Smith glanced impatiently at his watch. It seemed hours since she had walked down the steps with the canister. What in Christ's name was she doing down there? He looked at Johnny but saw no anxiety or impatience there. He envied Armstrong's calmness. The Luger hung loosely by his side and Smith knew that the confidence he so obviously placed in Marieanne's capabilities was one hundred per cent and could only have evolved over the years they had worked together.

All his early impressions of Johnny counted for nothing then and he doubted whether he had been right on any score. He was having great difficulty in deciding what the relationship between Armstrong and Marieanne was — apart from that of their profession. Smith felt cheated and, since Johnny had arrived on the scene, had been increasingly conscious that he was an outsider. He was jealous — and despised himself for experiencing such an immature emotion.

He was brought back to reality abruptly as the whole hall erupted into gunfire and death for a few seconds and he was witness to the incredible co-ordinated action of his two colleagues:

Marieanne entered quietly, followed by two men. With no pause for thought or word Johnny swung round, raised his gun, and fired. She fell flat on her face. The Jew immediately behind her seemed to be lifted off the ground; his revolver slipped limply from outstretched fingers, and a red patch spread out on his shirt. He was dead before he hit the ground.

Marieanne twisted round and kicked out at the other Jew's leg. He staggered but still fired. Smith saw Johnny's hands fly to his face; blood oozed between his fingers as he sank to the floor. Then she was on her back, right hand moving over her left wrist, pushing under the silk cuff. The Jew raised his gun at her but, before Smith could swing the sub-machine gun away from the others, her knife shot through the air. It sank to the hilt in the Jew's jugular vein, just below his ear. The canister he was holding crashed to the floor and he fired blindly, blood flooding his eyes. Tiles exploded into flying fragments around her but she rolled away from the ricocheting bullets before he fell, face down, over the canister.

El Dashiki saw the opportunity for escape and jumped at Smith, knocking him to the ground with a blow to the temple. He ran out through the door, followed by the three guards. Dazedly Smith stood up, ran to the door and fired a shaky blaze into the night. But the figures were lost against the shadows of the trees. He turned back.

Marieanne was on her knees by Johnny, who lay face down in a pool of blood. Carefully she turned him over.

'Oh my God, Johnny, no!'

His face was completely lost under the blood that ran down over his ears, soaking his hair and her dress and legs as she held him. Then she felt for his pulse and heartbeat.

'Is he dead?' Smith glanced at her while he kept his gun trained on the doctor and nurses who hadn't moved. One girl whimpered on the shoulder of the other.

'No,' she breathed and gazed emptily up at him. He saw the desperate fear on her face. She turned back to Johnny and called his name softly.

'He bloody well deserves to be dead,'

Smith railed bitterly. 'He nearly killed you!'

Marieanne had no spirit to answer and wiped blood from Johnny's eyes with an inadequate tissue.

'You didn't quite pull it off this time, did you?' he continued, then turned to the doctor.

'Get to work on him,' he ordered. 'You should be an expert at this sort of thing. And make a good job of it.'

He crossed over to Marieanne and crouched by her.

'I gather you'd feel lost without him?'

'He can't die,' she whispered.

'Well, my love, you can't expect your run of luck to last forever. The way you two go about your job it's inevitable that one, at least, is going to get killed eventually.'

He carried Johnny and followed Dr Khoury and the two nurses, who seemed considerably happier now that they had a patient. The doctor ushered them into a small room and Smith laid the unconscious body carefully on the bed.

After the nurses had cleaned Johnny's

face Dr Khoury examined him. Marieanne stood by Smith. She was pale and her fingers trembled and fiddled nervously with the buttons of her dress. It gave Smith a strange satisfaction to know there were chinks in her armour. At the same time it fanned his jealousy. She tried to peer over the shoulders that blocked her view but he pulled her back and they sat on the hard seats. The sub-machine gun lay over his knee. He leaned back against the cold wall and listened to the low Arab voices.

Eventually the doctor turned.

'He will be all right. The bullet ripped through his cheek then grazed past his skull.'

While they waited for Johnny to regain consciousness Marieanne took the canister back to the boiler room and ejected the bacteria into the incinerator. She felt no satisfaction; no pleasure that they had succeeded.

Then she walked slowly back up the stairs and into the room where Johnny was still unconscious. Smith left her covering Khoury and the nurses while he went to get Ali to drive the car up to the door.

She sat on the side of the bed, a Luger in one hand, her other hand stroking Johnny's forehead. He started to move and she called his name as the eyes flickered open. His left cheek and head were thickly bandaged. The flesh round his eye was swollen and bruising rapidly. For a few seconds he looked at her then groaned.

'Oh God, my rotten head hurts! What happened?'

His hands felt the dressings and he remembered pain blazing up the left side of his face, then nothing.

Marieanne told him. He closed his eyes and swore obscenely. Johnny was too narcissistic to stand facial disfigurement and his muzzy mind hunted through names of plastic surgeons. Then he sat up.

'Jesus, but you're a stupid fool at times, Marieanne. If you hadn't kicked him he'd have missed me by yards.'

His outburst brought on a fresh flow of blood that ran out of his mouth. One of the nurses immediately wiped it away and told him not to talk any more. He snatched the swab irritably and pushed her away.

Marieanne stared at him.

'You ungrateful wretch!' she began. 'If I hadn't kicked him he would have killed you at that range.'

Smith re-entered as Johnny was muttering into the blood-soaked swab.

'Stop complaining, Armstrong. She saved you from a cold slab in the morgue — and you know it.'

He pulled out his cigarettes — handed one to Marieanne then stuck one in Johnny's mouth which was immediately removed by the nurse.

'I know it must be sickening to have almost lost one side of your pretty face but our troubles aren't over yet.'

Marieanne looked up.

'Where's Ali?'

'It would appear El Dashiki and the guards got clean away,' Smith answered, ignoring her question.

'They couldn't have got far,' she argued. 'They had no transport. Hitchin, where's Ali?'

Smith laughed. The two nervous nurses looked at him suspiciously. Dr Khoury rubbed his smooth chin incessantly with his small fingers.

'Oh yes they had,' Smith went on, still ignoring her demands about Ali. 'There was a taxi waiting for them.'

'A taxi?'

Johnny fell back against the pillows.

'What a bloody farce!' he muttered.

Smith laughed again and the other two stared at him.

'What's the joke?' Marieanne implored.

'Ali obviously obeyed my instructions: the stupid bastard must have seen four people running out through the gates and picked them up.'

They all saw the joke but Johnny didn't laugh; he couldn't — it hurt too much.

10

Marieanne walked through the Communications Section, returning casual greetings with her office-bound colleagues, some of whom appeared to have never left their desks since she had first seen them — nine years before.

At the far end Johnny was leaning over a Telex machine. The young, curvy blonde behind it traced sympathetic fingers over his dressings, her face a study in adoration. Marieanne smiled, wondering what fantastic reason he was spinning for his injury.

'Good morning.' She tapped him on the shoulder. He turned and the blonde with the pink, English complexion looked up. Her hand fell back to the keyboard and she gazed enviously at the tanned, self-assured, and very beautiful Mrs Payne who, all the girls rumoured, was one of the code numbers they knew as agents.

'Don't believe one word of it,' she warned the girl in a loud whisper. 'He fell off a swing in the park.'

Johnny shrugged and they walked up to Sir John's office.

The Master was abrupt and irritable. He flapped the thick foolscap report, which they had spent the previous day typing, up and down in front of him. He pointed impatiently towards the chairs and looked from one to the other while they sat down and lit cigarettes.

The room was warm and Marieanne took off her embroidered, sheepskin Afghan jerkin from over the ribbed black sweater and pants. She folded it carefully on her knees and searched Sir John's face, but saw none of the pleasure and gratitude for a job well done.

His eyes turned back to the report and flicked the pages over while laboriously lighting his pipe. Then he sat back and the chair clanked painfully; the report slapped down on to the desk with so much force the contents of the ashtray scattered over various files and notepads.

'Well,' he finally began, 'neither of you

has emerged from this assignment in a blaze of glory: just the opposite, in fact.' His voice was acid. 'Maybe you have some suggestions as to how I can explain it away to the Minister.'

'I thought we did quite well,' Johnny protested, but the Master carried on.

'I sent Marieanne to do a job — a job which, I think, was no more difficult than many she has done in the past. And, to make things even easier for her, I sent you to help: you, Armstrong, who hold great hopes of sitting in this chair one day. So, knowing that my two top operators were working together, I felt entitled to be confident of a smooth, quiet, successful operation. Two Boy Scouts could have done better!' He pulled viciously on his pipe for a moment, glaring at their indignant disbelieving faces through the smoke. 'The only person,' he finally went on, 'to have come out of this Keystone Cop effort with any merit and dignity is Smith.'

Again he paused. The noisy pipe was out and he fished in a drawer for a new box of matches.

'It's unbelievable!' His big hand slapped down on the typed sheets. 'From Oxford to Beirut, and all over Lebanon, there's nothing but a trail of dead bodies. Both the Sûreté and Deuxième Bureau have been running round in circles trying to solve an unprecedented number of murders. You almost started a fresh outbreak of war between the Israelis and Arabs, then, to cap it all, you don't bring back the germs: you tell me they were destroyed in an accidental fire.'

There was another strained silence before Sir John continued to pile their sins of commission one on top of the other.

'And, by acting clumsily and impetuously, you *both* get wounded. You, Armstrong, will probably spend months languishing in a plastic surgery ward and expect full pay while you're there.'

He stood up. His birds were on the windowsill — the sparrows that gathered every morning for seed cake. Marieanne and Johnny were subjected to a blast of cold wind while he opened the window and fed them.

'We had no choice of action,' Johnny argued when the Master was back at his desk. 'The whole set-up in the Middle East is . . . '

'I'm quite well aware of the set-up in the Middle East, Armstrong — it keeps me awake at nights. However, it was no excuse for you to set yourselves up as a trio of trigger-happy terrorists.'

He sat down and eyed them imperiously, one finger tapping his chin, his eyes narrowing. The *coup de grâce* was about to be delivered.

'You're both going back for intensive re-training. Should anything serious turn up while you're away, I suppose I could send Smith to sort things out . . . '

Johnny swore under his breath. Marieanne looked across at him moodily and pulled at the wool of her jerkin.

' . . . Now I'll let you go away to lick your wounds.'

Again the report smacked against the blotter, but with a note of finality.

Marieanne glanced at her watch then crossed to the window. She looked down into the square below.

Johnny was behind her, his hand resting lightly on her shoulder.

'I'll run you home,' he offered. 'We can lick our wounds together for a few days — somewhere in the sun.'

They both saw the white Mercedes pull in behind his Citroën; the familiar rakish figure of Hitchin Smith climbed out and leaned against the bonnet.

Marieanne turned to Johnny and smiled.

'No thank you, darling, you've got to take it easy for a while. It can be quite serious having a bullet so close to your brain. Too much excitement could be very dangerous: I'd hate you to have a blackout.'

She bestowed a light, maternal kiss on his nose before walking away towards the door.

'Besides your critical condition, Johnny, I've already been invited to spend a few days in the sun.'

She left and tripped down the stairs as fast as her leg would allow.

Johnny watched from the window as she walked across the pavement, holding the brilliant jerkin close at her throat.

He smiled as Smith opened the door and helped her in. It began to rain as they drove out of the square.

THE END

We do hope that you have enjoyed reading this large print book.

Did you know that all of our titles are available for purchase?

We publish a wide range of high quality large print books including:
Romances, Mysteries, Classics
General Fiction
Non Fiction and Westerns

Special interest titles available in large print are:
The Little Oxford Dictionary
Music Book, Song Book
Hymn Book, Service Book

Also available from us courtesy of Oxford University Press:
Young Readers' Dictionary
(large print edition)
Young Readers' Thesaurus
(large print edition)

For further information or a free brochure, please contact us at:
Ulverscroft Large Print Books Ltd.,
The Green, Bradgate Road, Anstey,
Leicester, LE7 7FU, England.
Tel: (00 44) **0116 236 4325**
Fax: (00 44) **0116 234 0205**